Red Moon Rising

TRISTAN J. TARWATER

Book Design: Christopher Tarwater
Cover Artist: Amy Clare Learmonth
Editor: Annetta Ribkin

Print ISBN: 978-0-9840089-4-0

Dedicated to everyone still reading.

Prologue
Love Me, Tender

Tender noticed her as soon as she walked in. He set down the glass he was cleaning and watched as the young woman pulled back her hood, her dark eyes locking with his. He must have smiled at her because she smiled back, the din and bustle of the bar fading away as she approached him. It was more of a smirk, to be honest. As the young woman strode toward him she ran her fingers through her hair, pulling her dark, straight tresses over her ears, slipping past the occupied seats and tables of the establishment.

The young woman shrugged her pack off of her shoulders before she hopped up onto the stool, tucking her bag beneath her feet. Tender noticed the rough brown tunic she wore, her woman's belt tied with a white ribbon at the front. Tied at the front meant she was single. The barkeep placed a clay mug in front of her, pulling a jug of ale out from under the bar top.

"I'm thirsty," she said. Her voice bordered on husky, the tone and cadence of a girl from the city. Which city, he had no idea. Generally Tender kept bar and helped the town priestess run services. He rarely traveled far from his hometown of Whitend and mostly served drinks to locals, who were free to tell him their business over drinks or over prayers. He hadn't had a new face in town for two phases, and this customer...she smiled at him. Tender grinned, taken by the young woman sitting before him. Her full mouth parted slightly before she smiled. "What do you have to drink?"

Tender shook the jug he had just pulled up. "I've the house barley brew." He looked back at the wares on his shelf. Bottles of glass and clay, labeled and clean of any marks, lined the wall. "I've ground apple brandy made from last year's harvest," he started. "Thinny in six varieties, all made in my own cellars. Bluewine from the Southlands in three varieties, honey smacker from the base of the Holy Bowl and, well...milk, if you're interested." He meant the last bit as a joke. The new patron seemed a bit too young to be traveling on the borders of the Freewild alone; most people went in groups. Tender was hoping to get a rise out of her, as he wanted to see what happened to her mouth when it became angry. Instead, the dark traveler nodded, her eyes narrowing slightly.

"I'll have a mug of milk, please," the young woman said, leaning in a bit more, her voice lower, as if wanting a mug of milk was to be kept a secret. Was she pressing on him? The barkeep couldn't help but lean in as well, the sounds of the bar dampened by his lack of attention.

"Are you sure you don't want something else?" Tender asked. "Do you not find other...appetites lacking?"

The young woman cocked her head to the side and she rested her elbow on the bar top, chin on her hand. A smile sparkled in her dark eyes and she drew closer, taking the empty mug in her hand.

"I do, as a matter of fact. I'm sure you'd be able to help me out."

Tender felt his heart thump in his chest. Who was this woman who had just shown up in his bar? Someone called for him but he didn't care, at the moment. She smiled wider at him, her short, dark hair shifting so he could make out the slight point to her ear. A Forester? He thought she was a southerner, perhaps but the slight point was no mistake. What was this strange Forester doing in his bar, making eyes like this at him?

"And what might your name be?" she asked, a hint of curiosity playing in her voice. The barkeep laughed, finding himself not as famous as he thought.

"I'm Tender," he said. Tender turned around and grabbed the pitcher of milk he kept for the few patrons who wanted it. He waited for her to laugh but the traveler just nodded and watched him fill her mug. Her brow furrowed slightly as he poured the milk, looking up with a quizzical expression. He placed the pitcher back on the shelf and brushed his hair back with his hands. "And you?"

"I'm Point," she said after a moment, picking up her mug and tilting it toward her, looking down into her cup. Now Tender laughed, again ignoring the calls of someone in the bar.

"That hardly sounds like a real name," he said, walking around the counter. Tender decided to sit down next to her. The woman named Point watched him as he approached and eased back slightly as he took the seat beside her. She smelled good, he decided. Like leather and flowers and something spicy. Things he couldn't place, but they were pleasant all the same. Point leaned away from him slightly, taking her sweet scent with her, her mouth pulled in with a bit of disdain.

"My name don't sound real?" she asked. "And Tender does?"

Tender laughed, a loud, deep laugh that rang throughout the bar. "Tender is my real name," he chuckled. "My family name. Braxton Tender. I thought I was more well-known than that but…I guess not." He took her cup from her hands and took a sip of it, the white cream sticking to his mustache.

"Who's the owner of this establishment?" Point asked, shifting in her seat. Her voice became more businesslike, authority straightening out her spine. She was tall. Tender probably weighed as much as two of her, though.

"Well, I am the owner of this bar," he said, wiping his mustache clean with his hand. "I am the owner, as well as the tender, as well as a Tender. Is Point your personal name or your family name?"

The young woman turned her face away from him so all he saw of her was the back of her head. Her hair was a bit too short for his liking but it seemed to suit her face, her slender frame. Point finally turned her attention to him again, the same smile she'd originally had playing on her face, her dark eyes narrowed, long lashes framing them.

"It's a family name," Point said finally. The way she spoke dispelled any doubts Tender may have had about her name. She took her drink back from him, looking into it before bringing it to her lips, draining the contents in one gulp. She set the mug down on the bar top with a thump and sat straight on her stool, facing the bar once more and away from Tender. "Now," she said, with the same businesslike tone from before. "Could you get me a proper drink? I need one. Desperately."

Braxton rose from his chair to fulfill her request, taken aback by the subtle yet obvious change in the young woman. A sudden weariness had settled over her face, a weariness he didn't expect to see. "I've come a long way," she added, "and I still haven't found out where the temple is so I can say my morning prayers."

"This bar serves as the temple, Miss Point." Tender walked behind the bar again, looking over his bottles before he settled on the ground apple brandy. "People head to the Barony proper for festivals and White Night, but here, Sister Kella holds services in the bar, if she can manage to make the words. Mysteries she speaks, generally, from the bottom of a bottle or under a chair, though the gray robes still fit her well enough." The liquid gurgled as it swirled out of the bottle, dancing up the sides of the cup before settling, the sweet scent of last autumn's ground apples and liquor wafting up into the air. Tender corked the bottle and set it back in its spot, making a mental note to pull another one up from the cellar next time he was there. "I generally hold service, truth be told."

"You?" Point laughed. Dark, slender hands wrapped around the glass, beads from a prayer bracelet she wore clinking gently. She brushed her hair over her ear, the bemused smile staying on her lips as she took a sip, eyebrows raising as she swallowed. Tender watched as she shuddered slightly, obviously taken with the drink. Point licked her lips and looked up at him, her gaze again seeming to dampen the sounds of the tavern. "I doubt that," she mused. "Your tits aren't big enough to fill those robes and well...that seems silly to me. You hardly seem the priestessy type."

Tender's mouth dropped open, slightly surprised by her choice of words. "Maybe I am a priestess, in a veil, presented as a man. Perhaps the Goddess disguised me to aid me in my religious duties, to better serve her people. Did you ever think of that?"

"Or maybe she made you a man as a punishment," she offered, obviously not taking his words very seriously. "I'm sorry, but I'm going to have to drink quite a bit more to believe that. Actually, I'm not sorry. But I am in need of another drink." Tender looked down and indeed, the girl had somehow downed it, glass completely empty. She tapped the top of her cup, indicating he should fill it. "Besides," Point added, tilting her head to the side slightly. "You sound like a man. You talk like a man. And you've been eyeing me like a man. It's more likely the priestess is a drunk, as you say, and you've taken over her duties. To what end?" The young woman shrugged and tossed her drink back, swallowing half of it without flinching this time. She wipe her mouth with the back of her hand, tapping the top of the drink for yet another refill.

"The end is not the reason I do it, Miss Point, though I hope to do it till my end." Again, someone shouted his name. There was a crash from the left side of the bar and the sound of glass shattering. Point looked at him, an amused smile playing on her face as she listened to his words. "I tend bar and I tend to people because they need the pale light to illuminate the paths they choose to take. People have it hard enough without someone to confide in. After their drink and our talks if they feel brand new, let them go their way. If they feel like they need another go, there is always another bottle or another ear. Now," Tender said. He reached under the bar counter and pulled out a large wooden club, the end wrapped in fabric. "If you'll excuse me."

"Damn you, Halls, I told you to stop lording over people in my bar. Leave them be and be on your way, in the name of the peace and sovereignty!" With the threat shouted so loud the entire bar seemed to shake, Tender jumped onto the bar and down onto the man named Halls who barely had time to scream.

Chapter 1
Breaking New Ground

Tavera grabbed her drink and slid off her chair, sidestepping to avoid colliding with fleeing patrons. The solid smack of the padded club against a bare skull rang through the bar. She lazily slurped her drink while slipping a dagger out with her free hand, holding the blade upside down so the cool metal of the blade lay flush on her wrist.

Braxton Tender. Was he a tender or a priest? He was brawling with no less than three men. He picked up the man called Halls by his collar, readying another blow with his club. "I'll teach you to cheat people of their money," Tender yelled. Before Tender could teach Halls anything, a thug pushed a table into Tender from behind, hard. Tender stumbled forward, grimacing as he tripped and fell on top of Halls. The thug tried to upend the table on top of Tender but the bartender rolled away. He jumped up, club in hand, and rushed the thug. He feinted left, then right. A quick shot to the knee made the man's leg buckle under him, his face red with pain. The thug bellowed as he careened to the floor. In front of Tender stood the other thug, who had been waiting on the sidelines.

The sound of metal scraping against metal drew gasps from the remains of the crowd as a shortsword was drawn, a devilish grin lighting up the swordsman's face. Tavera knew the man was scared. Despite his grin, his grip was tight on its hilt. Tavera saw his knuckles were white.

"I'll cut you in two, Tender!" the man screamed. "Cut you in two and take your town!" The man swung forcefully, the club catching the sword just inches from Tender's face. The sharp blade ate into the wood. The sword stuck in the wood, much to the dismay of its wielder. When the man pulled to get it out, Tender let go of the club. The force sent the man wheeling back, hitting himself in the face with his own sword. Tender knelt down on top of him and punched the man in the face with a bare fist.

Tavera shifted her weight, draining her glass but keeping it in hand, watching the second man regain his footing and exchange punches with Tender. "I'll rid my town of you all," Tender shouted, a short, sharp groan spilling from his mouth as the man punched him across the chin. "By Her Bosom, the farmers don't need protection from the likes of you." He punctuated his words with the sick sound of knuckles against flesh and bone.

Tavera stepped closer but kept her back against the bar. She was used to being around brawls, though she had the sense to stay out of them. Down on the ground, the man reached for the shortsword, Tender kicking the sword away. Red in the face with anger and exertion, the man checked Tender at the knees instead, both of them crash-ing to the floor.

Halls stood up from where he had fallen, his eyes finally focused. Tavera saw the anger in his face, malice darkening his visage as he glared at the back of the barkeep. Another blade was drawn, this one bent and twisted looking, though the sentiment behind drawing such a blade was much nas-tier. Halls snarled as he gripped its hilt, raising his arm to strike his distracted foe.

Tavera smashed her cup into his skull, a rain of pottery shattering across the back of his head Shards of clay bit into her palm as she grabbed him by his hair. If the cup was not enough, surely the edge of the bar top would suffice. Catching Halls off balance, Tavera quickly turned him and pushed him face first into the bar. There was a significant "crunch" as the bridge of his nose buckled under the force. A shriek of pain shredded the air. The man crumbled to the ground, covering his now bleeding face with his hands.

The man who was on Tender looked to Halls, his face filled with dread. His expression turned to surprise and then pain when Tender punched him in the throat. All the thug could do was gag, clawing at his neck as Tender picked up the swordsman by the collar and the back of his pants, tossing him outside with a grunt. Tavera watched as he grabbed the choking thug and then Halls by the necks and dragged them both outside as well, the two men clearly defeated in body, if not in spirit.

Tavera stood in the doorway, watching the impressive shape of the bartender stand over them. A light, chilly spring rain was falling, dampening the shoulders of his shirt. She couldn't see Tender's face but already she could imagine it. The triumphant but calm expression, the peace in his eyes though he had just brawled with enemies. Even when Tender was being strangled, there had been no desperation in his face, no manic struggle to survive. Just determination to make happen what eventually did happen.

"You are unwelcome in my establishment," Tender said, spitting to the side. Claw marks on his neck dripped with blood. "Neither for drinks nor prayers. I will not have you pressuring farmers for your protection. I will not have you lying to impressionable folks for your own benefit. May you pull back your veils." He then turned around and walked back into the bar, apparently done with the pile of moaning men lying in front of his bar.

Tavera blinked as he walked past her. That's what this had been about? Extortion? "Wait," she said as she walked back into the bar, disbelief in her voice. "You fought those men because they were blocklords?"

Tender laughed, sauntering behind the bar. He pulled down two cups and a bottle, filling them. The bar seemed oddly quiet after the brawl. Bruised and bloodied fingers wrapped themselves around the glass and he tipped it back. A bit of it trickled from his bleeding mouth as he looked to her, smacking his lips. "Blocklords? Do you see any 'blocks' around here? These are more like stupid grip-grabbers who turn intimidation into a lifestyle. Parasites."

"Ain't the magistrate supposed to deal with criminals?" Tavera said, leaning up against the door frame. "Send the browncloaks after them?"

"No magistrate, not this year," Tender said, pouring himself another drink. "Whitend didn't make it into the Barony proper this Baron's Day. His horse suffered an injury in Redwell, so the territory was cut short this year, with me and my people outside of it. Not under the baron's sword and seat, so I've got to swing my club a bit more."

"His horse gets a lame leg, you get booted. It's a shame," Tavera said, sounding more cheerful than sympathetic. She had spent Baron's Day in the Freewild. The secular holiday was a day barons rode their horses as far as they could for one day. Every town, city and village within a day's ride was in the baron's territory and under their jurisdiction. Any land outside was the Freewild Green, a place of no rules. Early spring always saw a small migration of people to either order or chaos. Tavera knew this town was in the Freewild because of the lack of browncloaks but didn't know it'd been outed so recently.

Her boots sounded loud as she walked across the bar. Even in his bloodied state, Tender still eyed Tavera as if he wanted her more than the drink. She sat back down glad to see her pack undisturbed. "So what happened? The magistrate left and took all the browncloaks with him then?" A well-organized town with a decent bar and without guards? It wasn't the worst thing Tavera had come across in her days.

"One stayed," Tender offered, raising his eyebrows at her.

Tavera stared into her glass, thinking of Lori. She remembered the look on his face the night he had caught her in the middle of the take, the take which had ended in her getting into the Cup. Surprise in his light eyes, his dirty-blond hair under his helmet. His cloak stained with red. She remembered the feeling of pushing her sword into him, sinking into muscle, grating against bone. The pain in his eyes. Tavera shook her head, trying to push the memory away and wondering why the Goddess would sit her in front of another browncloak. Even a retired one.

"Someone's got to keep the order, I suppose," she mused, not sure who she was referring to exactly. It could have been Tender. Or Lori. Or even Derk.

Tender shrugged his broad shoulders. "I have the bar. And family. And the priestess to care for."

"Barkeep, priest, magistrate, browncloak," Tavera said, wrapping her fingers around the glass and gulping it down. "By Her paps, next you'll say you're the chawing midwife too." Tavera pushed her empty cup towards Tender, tapping it, indicating the barkeep should fill it again.

Tender laughed and filled her glass again, nodding at the door as a patron entered the bar. "No, that'd be Gera's specialty," he admitted. "I don't catch babies, just try to keep a bit of order so we can all be safe and lead happy lives.

Tavera propped an elbow on the bar top and put her chin in her hand. She sipped from her cup slowly, consider-

ing what he had just said. "So you've no one over you, save
the priestess. Just one priestess, correct?"

"Just the one," Tender nodded.

"But you not only stay and serve the town, but you kick
people out, if they don't follow the old laws?"

"I don't want them to leave, Miss Point," Tender said. He
sighed quietly, pouring the contents of the jug into his glass,
filling the cup all the way to the top and bringing the bottle
to his lips to finish it off. He set the empty bottle on the bar
before picking up his glass carefully. "I want them to stop
imposing their wills on the people of this area, so the people
of Whitend can make their own decisions. Tits," he said, a
few drips of the liquor spilling over the side as he spoke. He
took a gulp, his lips wet as he pressed them together before
continuing. "I'd prefer they realize cheating people out of
their money, time and energy will not help them on the
path to finding themselves. That it hurts people. Someone
has to guide them."

Tavera laughed out loud, turning her glass in her hand
as she stared down into its bottom, not able to keep her
smile from being dampened by cynicism. "Those are heavy
words coming from a barkeep," she finally offered. It wasn't
the first time she had heard deep words from a purveyor of
spirits but this was a bit much. She raised a brow at Tender,
noticing his mustache twitched slightly, as if her words
made it jump. Good. The half-elf brushed a lock of hair behind her good ear, dark eyes giving the tender a sideways
glance. "What if people want to cause harm? What if that is
their desire? To take advantage of people and attain their
higher goals by climbing up the backs of others?"

"Look, you're obviously from the city, so I won't fault
you for asking this," he said, the faltering she had seen there
gone as quickly as he spoke. "Life is busier there and there
are plenty of shiny things to distract those without resolve

or convictions. But if someone is given the choice to get something done by hurting someone or by not, what do you think they would choose?"

"It depends on which one is easier," Tavera said, trying to keep her words steady and managing. The choices he presented were so black and white, it seemed unrealistic to her. "You're making things out to be simpler than they actually are."

"So you're saying people hurt other people out of laziness?"

"I didn't say that!" she spat. His accusation bothered her more than his previous statement.. Tavera hadn't been angry at anyone in a while, not like this. The last person who had made her angry was Derk and it had been over some of her habits which she wasn't about to change. Though Tender didn't know it, he had insulted her and her way of life. It pricked her emotions. Tavera knew she led a life that left people a few coins or belongings short but she would never concede to being called lazy. It was hard traveling around, planning, avoiding the browncloaks. So was sitting still. It was difficult finding work she didn't find boring or monotonous. Tender seemed happy to tend bar, or at least he had when she had first walked in. Why couldn't Tavera be as happy at whatever she put her hand to?

Tender looked her over again, the same way he had looked at her before. It annoyed her. Tavera wished she had another drink but didn't want to ask for one just yet. "You can't tell me you sincerely believe every single person on this earth would do what you think is the right thing if they could. What you consider to be right."

"I can and I do," he said. He turned toward the back of the bar, pulling a bottle of beer from the shelves and uncorking it, setting it in front of her. Tavera narrowed her eyes. "All people can find their destiny, but it must be actively sought. Your path'll be hindered by piles of bodies and people chasing after you. Guilt, fear, envy, all those things are man-made veils which hide who we really are. It's basic doctrine."

"You think very highly of people." Tavera brought the glass bottle to her mouth and took a pull off of the drink, the wheat beer a bit too sweet for her liking, but drinkable. Her words hadn't been meant as a compliment, the tone of her voice implying she was giving him a warning. Tavera froze in her seat, hearing the voice of her father in her head speaking in those same tones. The thief swished the gulp of beer around her mouth and swallowed the thoughts down, continuing before Tender could give a rebuttal.

"So that's it, then?" she started. "Leave people to their decision making and all you have to do is bang a few heads together to help them on their way? Literally, knock some sense into some bad folk. I'm sure every single bad person will pass through for a mug on their way to their kidnapping and killing parties."

The man just blinked, his eyes focused on her, his hands steady on the bar top. Tavera guzzled the beer, wondering if he was going to charge her for this, but also waiting for his response. She hadn't meant to make him feel stupid. His thought process was interesting and almost beautiful. Had she not seen and experienced half of what she had in her life, she could have maybe given him some credence.

Instead she finished her beer and hopped off the stool, setting the empty bottle before him. Tavera tried to smile but couldn't. A pang of guilt swam in her stomach. Tender looked at her mouth and then stared into her eyes, his face still managing to hold the same conviction in his gaze and features.

"You are jaded," Tender said finally, eyes still locked with hers.

"I don't know what that means, but you're naïve," Tavera replied. She quickly refastened the clasp of her cloak, her clothing hidden by the heavy, dark material as it draped over her slight frame. She pulled her cap out of her back pocket and pulled it over her head, tucking her hair away before she picked up her pack and slung it over one shoulder before turning back. "Now, if you'll excuse me, I must be on my way out of your town. Orphans to stab and such. Old ladies to deflower."

"Where are you going?" The emotion in his voice seemed misplaced. Hadn't they just been talking the morality of those in the Valley? Tender called after her as if his life depended on her staying. Tavera spun around slowly on one heel till she faced him once more. Perhaps she should work this.

"I've already told you. Orphans. Stealing." She let her face imply she was joking though she spoke in only half-jest. She knew his interest was piqued, that he was curious about her. Tender was the leader of the area, religious and moral. This was probably the only tavern for a good stretch. It was just on the outskirts of the Barony, bordering the Freewild. She had just crossed the Freewild and had thought to turn south and see if she could find Lights. But she was here, now, with the ex-browncloak. The way he had asked after her made her want to stay.

Perhaps he felt some kind of moral obligation to keep track of her, in addition to physical interest. Tavera never felt in the mood to have long, drawn-out conversations about the natural state of people and their destinies; she was more eager to find her own. Trying to convince Tender he was wrong wasn't something she necessarily wanted to do either. But to have the unofficial leader of the area on her side might not be a bad thing.

"You are joking," he stated, brushing his hair back with his fingers. "There are no orphans who are unaccounted for here. There's actually not much to do here except pass through. So, are you headed into the Wild or to the Barony proper?"

"You know, I ain't certain," Tavera lied. Halfway to the door she could tell Tender was agitated. "Maybe the Green," she said with a toss of her head. "I ain't been in a while and there's always something fun to do there."

"It's dangerous in the Green."

"Didn't I just say there was fun things to do there?" Tavera crossed her arms over her chest and tilted her head to the side. "I'm not one to sit about protecting farmers."

"But you are one to help out in a fight, aren't you?" Tender's eyes glinted and he smiled somewhat knowingly, as if he thought he had hit something. Tavera laughed, turning around slightly so she could see the door, wondering if she should in fact make her exit or stay on. He had baited her, or so he thought. What did she want to do?

"Maybe I just know the best side of a fight to be on," she offered. This wasn't entirely false.

"The best side is the right side," Tender said. A smile broke under his mustache, hope in his eyes. It made Tavera nervous. She wrapped her arms around herself tighter and leaned back toward the door, toward the way out.

"I really should go," she said. "Besides, if you succeed in your goal of making all the townspeople good, I'll most likely be the one with a dirty face." Tavera felt her expression grow more somber, though she didn't mean it to. That was the truth of it. If she stuck around, she might wind up tossed out of Tender's bar or town, or having to sneak out. She couldn't fault him for wanting to keep the peace for the good of the people, not his pockets. Tavera didn't really want to be chased out of town, not just yet. The thief turned toward the door, the thought of heading south in her head.

"I could help you get cleaned up."

This was a little much. Tavera turned toward him, her dark eyes wide with warning, her arms still folded across her chest. She cleared her throat before she shook her head.

"I believe the saying is, 'She holds the torch but we must walk.' Is this not true, Tender of drinks and destinies?" She smiled wryly at him. "It's also a bit…stupid to assume I need your help. I mean, I was the one who smashed that man's face in."

"Stay for a phase. You obviously want to stay, or you would have left before this conversation even started." His eyes shone, perhaps with too much drink. The blood which had been bright red on his split lip was scabbing over, the bruises on his face and neck starting to turn purple. He looked so pitiful and so genuine in his wanting her to stay. What would Derk advise her to do?

Derk would tell her without a plan she'd be blown anywhere. Best to sit and stew for a bit; thoughts are best simmered before served. He would wag his eyebrows at her and roll a cigarette too. Whitend was the first place someone had asked her to stay in a very long while. If there was no danger in staying, it would be better to figure out her next move within walls than without. She had come here in the hopes of finding someone from the Cup to help her; someone without any ties to her or an agenda might be better.

"If I did want to stay," she suggested, rocking back and forth on her heels, "where could I stay? Not a barn. Or a basement neither."

"Well, not to add another profession to my list, but I tend the inn," Tender said. "I rent a few rooms upstairs. You could stay in one. I just got a vacancy." The barkeep looked past her toward the door leading outside, the lack of moaning implying the men who had been lying there had left. "How about it?"

"What makes you think I have any money?!" Tavera laughed, her amusement genuine. Tender looked at her quizzically. She caught her breath and wiped a tear from her eye. "You're a good one, telling me I have to stay and then

charging me to do so. Tits, I'll be on my way, then. Toss off."
This time she really did head toward the door, disappoint-
ment pulling at her mouth as she put her hand on the door.
Is that what this had been about? Profit?

"No, wait! I mean...." Tavera looked over her shoulder at
him, hand still on the door. There was a bit of panic in his
eyes, desperation. He awkwardly pointed toward the stairs
which most likely led to the rooms he had been talking
about. "Look, you can stay in a room for the phase, no
charge. I'm sorry, that was rude of me. It's just..." he paused,
his brows and mustache furrowing with confusion. "Well,
how were you expecting to pay for your drinks, if you had
no money?"

"I always get someone else to pay. That's what I do."
Tavera let the front door close and walked over to the stairs,
a hop in her gait. Drinks and a room. Pretty good for herself
with just a few words and breaking a man's face. She looked
at Tender and saw he was mystified. He didn't look put off
by it, just intrigued. How far could she push it? "I don't ask
for favors, I garner them. Now which room is it?"

"Uh...third one, no...second on the left. It's unlocked."

"And I assume your town has a bathhouse?" she asked,
cocking her head to the side. "Ayilkin folk, former and cur-
rent, like to keep clean, I hear? I've been on the road and I
could use a soak."

"It's five doors down, in the old barn, but it's two blues
for the water, one for each heating stone," Tender said, furrowing his brows.

"Well then, I've an offer you can't refuse," Tavera said,
tossing her pack onto the bar top and opening it up. She
pushed past the neatly folded clothes and found what she
was looking for, tied in a pile. "You look like a man who
could use a hanky. Always getting into scrapes, working up
a sweat, hitting people in the face."

"Are you making fun of me?" Tender asked. Tavera smirked as she splayed the pile of handkerchiefs out so he could see the designs.

"No, I'm trying to get you to buy one of these fine hankies so I can pay for a bath," Tavera said, looking over the embroidery on the edges. "Good for mopping a brow, wiping up blood. Well, the dark ones are good for wiping up blood. I think this one, though," she said, picking up one of the delicate fabric squares and folding it, holding it up to his face. It was a pale blue with white embroidery of moths on it. "I think for sheer handsomeness, this is the best." Tavera picked among the assortment and held up another one, this one a dark blue. "This is the one to get bloody."

"You make these?" he asked. There was something much like surprise in his voice.

"Of course," she said. Tavera had stolen the fabric and Gam had embroidered them. In a way she had made them. "I'll sell you both of these I picked, special for you for...five blueies."

"Five blueies!" he asked, laughing. Tavera decided she liked Tender's laugh. He laughed a lot, even with bruises darkening on his face.

"Alright, three for five, that's my final offer and if you don't take it, I will ruin your sheets when I lay in them, I will," Tavera shot quickly, rifling through the hankies and pulling out a dark brown, almost black one with green embroidery of leaves on the corners. "Look, I'm even picking this other one, look how dark it is. That's a long soak in the dye, better quality."

Tender chuckled, his laugh higher pitched than his voice. She would have taken the time to think about how charming it was if she wasn't trying to make a few coins. Tender reached behind the counter and pulled out five coins, laying them on the bar top. "Five for the three?"

Tavera handed the hankies over and took the coins, tucking them away before she put the unsold wares back into her pack. "Just don't tell anyone about the deal I gave you. Never know how much I can make off the rest of them." Tavera smiled and bowed, trying not to laugh as he blinked at her. Before he could say anything she popped up the stairs, taking them in twos and counting the doors be-fore she opened the one leading to the room the barkeep had said she could take.

Fresh sheets. A clean mattress, raised off the floor, even. A small table with a chair. The key for the room hung from a leather cord tied to the inside door ring. Tavera took it and wrapped it around her wrist as she closed the door with a kick. Country people knew how to treat guests, paying or not, that was for sure.

Tavera threw her pack to the floor and flopped on top of the bed, the sheets cool on her face. She would sleep well tonight. It would be nice to have a pillow to cry into, she mused. She scoffed at herself as she sat up on the bed. No time for self-pity. She was just tired. Less than two phases ago she had been inducted into the Cup. Now she was on the opposite side of the Valley, wondering what the Hems had happened.

Derk had been put in the Jugs. He'd told her when she was in the Cup, she would always have someone to fall back on, someone to help her out and it hadn't been the truth. News of one of them getting pinched and they scattered like spring blossoms in one of the last breezes of winter. Even Gam wasn't in Portsmouth. Tavera had waited around her house like a dog, sitting on her stairs, leaning against the building, shivering. She'd finally got sick of waiting and looked east and south.

Lights was south, she knew that. He stuck to Mielkin and Sedrakin baronies. If she found him, they'd sort out something. Maybe things were just flipped over in the northern baronies.

But Tender. Tavera sighed and opened her pack, looking through it for a clean tunic. She shook her head as she thought about their conversation, what he had said. She recognized the expression in his eyes when he looked at her. But there was something else. The way he looked at everything. People were naturally good, Tender thought. While she didn't think this was true in any way, she didn't want to tear his strange worldview apart. There was something comforting in his face, a nobleness she didn't want to see scarred. At the same time, Tavera couldn't believe people were naturally good. In her experience, people naturally looked out for themselves and if they were lucky or unlucky, they did so for some loved ones as well.

Tavera pulled britches and a pair of socks out of her bag and folded them carefully. The sound of rain starting to fall outside made her feel even wearier but the idea of a soak in the hot water got her off the bed and out the door. She locked it behind her before she listened at the top of the stairs. Apparently enough time had passed; the sound of patrons talking and glasses clinking together could be made out from the upper level. Quietly she walked down the stairs, knowing she'd have to walk across the bar and Tender's line of sight to get out. Oh well. Nothing to be done about it.

Tavera walked down the landing and into the bar, making for the door with a nonchalant kind of urgency, measured and slow and obviously not caring about anything else happening in the bar. Out of the corner of her eye she saw Tender look up and before he could say anything, she shot him a glance and a smirk, acknowledging him. He just smiled. She noticed he had cleaned up.

Tavera pushed upon the door and sucked in the cool spring air, the rain not coming down hard enough to bother walking quickly. It felt nice and would only make the hot bath even better. She noted the spots in the mud where Halls and his men had been thrown, chunks of grass ripped up from the earth and the men nowhere to be seen. Probably headed deeper into the Freewild to cause real mischief. She sniffled and made her way to the house Tender had said was the bathhouse, taking long strides in the springtime rain.

Chapter 2
Trades and Acquaintances

Tavera threw the knife. Quicker than she could blink it whizzed through the air and sunk into the tree trunk. She sniffed in disappointment; the blade was outside the ring she had drawn on the trunk in charcoal. Tavera pushed back her failure and pressed on, weighing the next dagger in her hand. She wrapped her fingers around the tip of the blade, feeling the sharp metal which would eat into the wood. Don't flick your wrist, she told herself, licking her lips.

A spring breeze rustled the branches of the tree she was aiming for. Lunch and cards had been fun. Tavera had won a meal and a bit of laughter from some locals of Whitend. Now she was trying to grab some time to herself and practice throwing knives. Growing up, she'd heard of people being able to shoot daggers from their hands. People who could throw knives occasionally showed up in Derk's more unbelievable stories. But Tavera had actually seen a man throw knives in a little town on the west side of the Valley, before she headed east. He used special daggers, smaller than normal, their hilts just a smooth, weighted extension of the blade. Tavera had lifted her first throwing dagger out of the body the man had left behind and traded for another two. Tavera let the second dagger fly, trying to keep her wrist straight.

The dagger emitted a low thud as it sank into the wood. Tavera smiled with pleasure but didn't waste time, switching the remaining dagger to her right hand. She weighed it, feeling the grooves in the metal. She wanted to be able to throw all three in quick succession and have them hit the target, or at least close. Just as Tavera was about to let the dagger fly, the sound of footsteps made her ear perk up. She stepped sideways, a bit more off the road as she saw a figure approach out of the corner of her eye.

Judging the stranger to be a ways off yet, Tavera readied the dagger once more, eyes on the target. Tavera let the third dagger loose, this one bouncing off the last one she had thrown with a clang.

"Hems," Tavera cursed, pursing her lips and walking toward the tree to retrieve her blades. She turned her head to see who was coming out of the woods and waved a quick hello. He seemed about her height, with the kind of skin which shouldn't be out in the sun too much but evidently had been. Hair the color of straw stuck up on his head in different directions and his bare arms looked like ropes. Tavera squinted and saw the backs of his arms were covered in freckles. What pulled the smile from her eyes was the sword at his hip and the bow slung across his back. Most likely he used them on things like rabbits; a pair of them hung from his belt. She wrapped her fingers around her dagger, eyes still on him and she yanked, jerking it out of the tree.

He couldn't be much older than her, Tavera judged. Something around the eyes looked familiar to her. He nodded to her in greeting, looking over at the tree. He furrowed his brows and wrinkled his nose at Tavera, an unflattering expression on his face. "You shouldn't be throwing them daggers at the trees."

Tavera raised an eyebrow at him and flipped one of the daggers in her hand as he looked her over. Evidently he was trying to figure out who she was. "Why not?" she asked. "I'm trying to better myself, pick up a new trade. The Traveling Caravan of the Three Sisters needs a new knife thrower and I'm hoping to get picked up by them. If I don't practice, how will I ever get in? Unless you need a knife thrower here in Whitend," she offered, cocking her head. "Of course, if you don't want me practicing on this tree," Tavera turned on her heels and held the knife out toward the tree and then turned slowly toward the man, the tip of her tongue slipping past her lips as she pointed the blade toward the man. "You're...about...as wide as the tree. We could make this work."

"Moths for brains," the man muttered, pulling away from her and averting his eyes. He spit to the side and walked off toward the town proper, looking over his shoulder once as she watched him go.

"You're no fun! You've got no ambition!" she called after him with a laugh. Tavera slid the blade into her hands and hurled it at the tree, listening as it sank into the wood. A satisfied smile crept across her mouth. She retrieved the knife and tucked the small blades back into her boots and the other into her sleeve.

It was nice to have the weapons close to her body, easily hidden and always on her. Her shortsword was tucked away most of the time. It wasn't needed for every job. Useful but a specialized tool. Walking around with a sword made one a target. It was something to be checked in at some gates, not allowed in some establishments. Daggers on the other hand were easily hidden. Useful for cutting off the leg of a rabbit or threatening someone. Daggers were better at creeping along where skin rested over veins, she thought. No flourish, no brandishing. To the point.

Tavera couldn't help but pull out the dagger and flip it over in her hands. Maybe she could learn how to juggle knives. People always paid to see things like that. She had worked at a tea and spice shop when she was younger and knew a bit about tinctures and brews. But she wasn't sure how much a traveling tea merchant and spicer could make. The old shop used to get shipments in from all over the Valley and had a garden outside the wall providing it with common items. Tavera wasn't planning on disturbing any earth any time soon unless it was with her own two feet on her way out. Staying put and sowing didn't suit her. Besides. Throwing knives was fun.

The blade fell into her hand, flat, easy. She passed by houses, fields and gardens as she walked, waving to people working outside. Tavera saw an old man smoking a pipe on his porch while a few children played at his feet. Evening meal aromas wafted through the air, stews and soups and even a roast permeating the spring breeze. She would get something to eat at the bar after the service. Barley and lentils and spring greens mixed together with a mug of beer, the thickest Tender had.

Tender. Tavera smirked to herself. He was a decent cook and an exceptional brewer. He kept a clean set of rooms and was generally helpful to the denizens of Whitend. She turned a corner and stopped short, almost surprised to see the blond man with the rabbits and Tender talking outside the bar. Tender frowned, his mouth thin under his bushy mustache. Tavera noted the similarity around the eyes between the two, and even in the nose. The ears were different though. It wasn't just the piercings the rabbit man had. His ears were bigger. They probably turned red when he was embarrassed.

The rabbit man held the carcasses out toward Tender and Tender backed away, pointing toward the back door of the bar. The rabbit man lowered his head and shook it, glancing at the forest. It seemed Tender was trying to get him to go into the bar but something was keeping the other man from doing so. They talked back and forth for a few more breaths, the rabbits swinging from the man's hands.

Tender finally threw his hands in the air and took the rabbits, holding them away from him as if not to ruin his clothes. The rabbit man pulled away, walking back toward the forest or at least away from the bar. "Love you, Little," Tender called after him. Little called something back that Tavera couldn't make out and continued down the road. She saw Tender's shoulders drop as he watched the man leave before slowly entering the bar.

Tavera turned to leave as well and jumped, finding herself face to face with Priestess Kella. The priestess reeled back, eyes wide. Tavera laughed nervously, her face growing hot. "Afternoon, Sister," she purred, hands behind her back. "You headed to the bar to get ready for services?"

The priestess frowned. Her long, dark hair was pulled back in a messy bun, her robes slightly wrinkled. The odor of alcohol wafted from the holy person, incense and booze telling Tavera she had probably been praying and drinking. Sister Kella looked close to being past her child-bearing years but creases on her face and years at the bottle made her look older. Something had happened to her when she was younger, Tavera was sure of it. Sister Kella seemed too sad and at her age the priestess should have been serving in a temple further into the territory, or at least with a few priestesses under her. Instead she was in Whitend, with position and no power. Just a helpful, perhaps overzealous barkeep who provided her with a steady hand and a steady supply of alcohol.

"No," Sister Kella snorted. "I'm watching you."

Tavera cocked a brow. "Are you, now? Why might that be?"

"Boredom," Kella coughed. "I've seen Mam Karya churn her butter so many times, it's lost its excitement." Kella started walking past the trees, down the road, Tavera trailing beside her. "I've seen everything here, over and over. Garwin killing his chickens. Herika making her brew. Little bringing in his catch. Tender, with his arms crossed, watching over it all." Kella reached within her robes and pulled out a flask, unscrewing the top. "You're the most exciting thing to pull through here since we were booted from Ayilkin."

Tavera nodded, hearing the mention of Little. After two days in the small town, it was the first time she had seen him or heard mention of him. Curious as she was, she wasn't about to ask outright. "Most people like a predictable life, Sister," Tavera offered. She found the knife she had slipped into her jacket and turned it over in her hand. "Hasn't the Goddess set things in motion, routines, that we might learn from patterns?"

"Eh, patterns are for sewing dresses," Sister Kella drawled. "I could use a change of work and garment. I'll give you the robes and you give me the knife and hood."

"Sister, I would not give you a knife," Tavera chuckled. "Just as you would not trust me with your robes."

"So you don't trust me?" Sister Kella said. She took another swig from her flask.

"I don't know you," Tavera said, turning the knife over again. "I mean, you're a priestess. You know how to pray and light incense. What would you do with a knife?"

"What if I needed it for protection? Ever think of that?" Sister Kella humphed, closing her flask and putting it back in her robes. Her eyes were watery and bloodshot.

"Tell you what. If you need protecting, you tell me or Tender. We'll sort it all out, Sister," Tavera smiled. Something about the priestess' face puzzled Tavera. It worried her. The smile dropped from her mouth.

"You'll leave. They always leave," Kella muttered. "Except when you don't want them to, then they stick, don't they?"

Tavera narrowed her eyes at the priestess, the woman's cynical words sounding like something Tavera would have heard on the streets, not from a robed holy woman. Her thoughts turned to Derk and how he had been taken from her, and her promise to him, which she regretted now. Tavera remembered his face when he had asked her in the temple those years back. He made her promise if he was ever caught, she would not try to rescue him, but run away and live her life. She had said yes without thinking too much about it. It had been a holiday after all and there were boys to dance with and drinks to imbibe and purses to steal. Her heart still ached when she thought of Derk. If Tavera had her way, Derk would be with her still. But he wasn't, was he?

Tavera flipped the knife over in her hand again, trying to focus on the blade and not the feeling in her chest. "Who's sticking to you, Priestess?" she asked. "Who do you want to shake off?"

Sister Kella stopped in her tracks. Her worn and weary face told Tavera she wanted to answer. Her tears told even more. Tavera pressed her lips together and held the knife in her hand. She held it toward her, hilt first, offering it to the older woman.

The priestess stared at the blade. For a breath, Tavera considered pulling it back before the priestess could take it. Sister Kella looked from the knife to Tavera and back to the knife again. Finally Sister Kella shook her head and she backed away a few steps, shame in her gaze. "I really can't," the priestess murmured. "I shouldn't ask for your knife." The priestess blushed as she took yet another step back. "I should go. Prayers are soon, I must get ready."

"Right," Tavera said, still eyeing the priestess. She blinked and then tucked the dagger away, noting the priestess' eyes following the blade the whole way. "I'm off to Tender's to try and get a drink before the bar is turned into a temple."

"Gotta spend your gambling money somewhere, eh?" the priestess asked. Her eyes sparkled a bit, her mood seemingly lifted.

"Better I spend it here than in the Valley proper," Tavera grinned. "Besides, I gotta make money somehow. I've no trade or skill."

"Except gambling," the priestess snorted. "And lying. I'm sure you've something else up your sleeve. A real name, perhaps?"

"Just knives, sister," Tavera replied, bowing her head at the priestess' accusation. "One and the same, am I right?"

"I'm sure you often are." The priestess chortled and bowed her head in farewell, heading off in the direction of the little house where she stayed. Tavera watched her, wondering why the priestess hadn't taken the knife.

Chapter 3
Personal Qualms

Inside the tables were pushed aside to the sides of the room, stacks of chairs scattered through the room. Tender and one of the young women carried a table to the side to clear the floor to make room for worshipers. A few patrons straggled at the moved tables or bellied up at the counter, nursing their drinks and wrapping up games. Tavera raised a brow as Tender's eyes fell upon her, following her as she crossed the room and made her way behind the bar. Tavera smiled as demurely as possible at Tender, his face pinched with annoyance. "I'll be right back," he said to the woman, setting down his side of the table before he headed toward Tavera.

"What'll it be?" she asked, picking up a glass and setting it on the counter. "You look thirsty, Tender, you do, so let Point get you a drink."

"Please get out from behind my bar," he said. The barkeep sounded irritated. "Please."

"Well--"

"Please."

Tavera stifled a nervous laugh and raised her hands up in surrender. Tender strode past her, switching places. Once behind the counter the barkeep seemed more relaxed. He picked up the cup Tavera had set down. "Now," he said, the typical joviality returning to his face. He smiled at Tavera. "What can I get you?"

"I didn't want to bother you, is all," Tavera offered, hopping up on a stool. "I know you'se getting ready for prayers. Don't want the supplicants to start late on account of my being thirsty."

"Getting the drinks is my job," Tender reminded her.

"And this is your establishment, after all," Tavera reasoned, drumming her fingers. The thought that she had no place to call her own bothered her but there wasn't time to dwell on the fact. "Well, since I've got you here," she sighed, looking over the bottles on the back wall, avoiding Tender's focused gaze, "just a bottle of your dark," she decided.

"Dark drink for a dark lady," Tender joked, turning to get the bottle.

Tavera considered snapping back at him but couldn't think of anything to say. She folded her arms and watched as Tender uncorked the bottle and set it in front of her. Tavera shot him a look of disapproval as she brought the bottle to her lips, taking a swig. It was thick and malty, with fine bubbles that made it creamy. "It's a good beer," she said. "Your recipe?"

"My mam's," Tender said quietly. For a breath he just stood there, staring at the ground. Tavera took another gulp. "Oh, that'll be two blueies."

"Just add it to my room tab," Tavera said.

The corners of Tender's smile dropped and he put his hands on the counter top. "Your room...Miss Point--"

"Something added to nothing is still something, Tender," Tavera said, taking a step away from the bar, holding the beer bottle in both hands. "It's simple figures. Most people can sort it."

"So you're giving me permission to charge you for the drinks?" Tender asked.

"Well, I figure you know what I've got in my purse and know I'm good for it, why not get your grip of blues when you can?" she asked, watching Tender try not to blush. "I know you've got people keeping watch on me," Tavera shot. "How much've I got in my purse, Tender? You guess right, I'll pay you double for the beer."

"I guess right and you pay me double?" He stroked his mustache and smirked. "Sounds like a bet I can take."

"And when you lose, I get this beer for free," Tavera said, holding the beer up and taking another swig. She wanted to take it up to her room and savor it before prayers but a bit of fun and getting the beer for free wouldn't be a bad way to spend her time.

"Fine," Tender said. He looked her over, as if the answer to his question would be written on her somewhere. Tavera wagged her brows at him, letting her mouth hang open stupidly as he stroked his chin. "Eight blueies."

"Free beer!" Tavera exclaimed, throwing her hands in the air and almost spilling some of her gains in the process. Tender made a sound that was half a laugh, half a curse as he turned away from her. The young woman who had helped him set up the bar for service handed him two chairs, laughing at Tender as well. He sighed and set the chairs in place, starting the first row for would be worshipers.

Tavera leaned back on the bar and thought about her purse. It had five in it, and her second purse had three but she always kept a few coins tucked into her belt. Eleven altogether. Quite a bit for a few hands of cards in a small town but Tavera wasn't complaining. Tender had underestimated her.

Tavera took another sip from her beer and shook her head at the barkeep, watching him set up chairs. "You didn't think the priestess would be best at keeping eyes on me, did you? You should send that handsome fellow after me next time, unless you're trying to keep him all for yourself." She enjoyed the puzzled look on Tender's face, watching him trying to figure out who she was talking about. "Is he your lover?" she asked. "He ain't going to be happy when I tell him the eyes you've been making at me."

Tender shook his head. The young woman laughed. "Lovers? This one? He's too busy standing with his arms crossed to do anything with anyone."

Tender shot a look at the woman, placing his hands on his head. He was obviously a bit embarrassed by the comment and he cleared his throat. "That's not all I do, Bayla," he shot at the young woman before turning his attention back to Tavera. "No, uh…I mean, who are you speaking of?"

"Blond hair, big ears, too serious for his own good?" Tavera said. "Good at catching rabbits?"

Tender laughed out loud, smiling. "Who's watching who?" Tender asked, setting up a few more chairs. "That's my brother, Little. Herix, but everyone calls him Little." Tender spun a chair under his hand before he set it in its place, smirking a bit at Tavera. "Why, were you jealous?"

"No, I've never wanted a sibling," Tavera quipped, taking a sip of her beer. Brothers? She recalled the other man's face. There was a similarity there. But Tender was dark-haired with a darker complexion while Little had hair the color of hay and freckled under the sun.

"You know what I meant." Tender walked behind the bar. He bent down and when he stood up he had a guitar in his hands. He pulled a strap out and came back around.

"Jealous that you're not sleeping with your brother?" Tavera watched as he latched the strap to either end of the guitar and pulled it over his head. Broad fingers pressed into the strings and he strummed a happy chord, plucking a few notes, turning the keys as he tried to get the instrument in tune.

"Forget I said anything," he insisted, continuing to play. "Are you coming to service?"

"Planning on it," Tavera said. "Though I prefer morning prayers to vespers."

"Somehow, I'm surprised to hear you're a morning person," Tender said, strumming a few quick chords and taking off the guitar. He ran his hand across the counter before he laid the instrument on top.

"I'm not," Tavera admitted. "I usually stay up all night, go to morning prayers and then go to bed."

Tender grinned at her. "Some things do change, I guess."

"For now," Tavera said, smiling but narrowing her eyes at him. She took another sip and looked to the guitar, noting its craftsmanship. "Where'd you get the guitar?"

"Oh, it was my father's," Tender said. "He left it here, years ago. My mam gave it to me when I was big enough to hold it."

"Did he leave anything for your brother?" Tavera asked. She stared at the top of her drink, waiting for Tender's answer.

"A hunting knife, actually," Tender said. He picked up a chair and moved it over. "Which suits him. Guess he knew."

"Right," Tavera said. She thought about this for a breath before she sighed, turning to head up the stairs. "Well, I'm off to my room for a bit. How long after vespers is evening meal?"

"I started a stew this afternoon, as I usually do on days we hold prayers, but we'll have drunk rabbit and cakes if you're willing to spend your hard-earned money." Tender wagged his eyebrows at her as she backed toward the stairs.

"What kind of stew?" she asked, her back toward the door leading to the staircase.

"Duck with white tops and greens and mushrooms," Tender said.

"Any sausage in it?" she interrogated.

"No." Tender looked confused.

"Good," Tavera said. "I hate sausage. I'll see you at prayers." With a nod of her head, she slipped up the stairs, down the small hallway, ducking into her room. She locked the door before she set the beer on the small table and flounced onto the bed.

Staying up during the day was hard, she told herself, laying on her back. Tavera reached out and grabbed hold of her beer bottle, taking another mouthful. It was good beer. The best she'd had? It was a tossup. More interesting than the beer was the priestess and Tender. What had happened to Sister Kella to warrant her strange position in the village? The priestess didn't seem too upset about it. She obviously had other things in her mind.

Tender's brother also interested her. It seemed almost obvious they didn't have the same father but Tender hadn't mentioned it. Not that it mattered. Tender was obviously devoted to his brother. The barkeep was obviously a man of loyalty, probably to a fault. It was a curiosity which piqued Tavera's interest and it made the prospect of heading south to see Lights a little dimmer. Never bad to learn something about where you are, that's what Derk would say. She could find out more about the priestess and see just how far Tender's devotion went before getting on the road. Tavera took another gulp of her beer and set it back on the table, pulling her prayer beads off the stand and wrapping them around her wrist.

She'd had it in her mind to lie in bed before service but now Tavera felt restless. A walk around town would probably calm her nerves. She raked her fingers through her shaggy dark hair before pulling her cap back on, tucking in the loose strands, hiding her ears away. A shawl would keep away the chills on her stroll and if the windows were opened during the service, which they should be. It let the prayers of the people and the incense of the altar spill out into the open air, or so the sermon said. Tavera wondered who made the incense for the church and where Tender and Sister Kella kept it.

Bringing her bottle, her prayer beads and her purse with her, Tavera exited the room. She turned and carefully tucked a ribbon between the door and the frame, making sure no one else was in the hallway and it couldn't be seen while standing in front of the door. Her boots clomped down the stairs, loose on her ankles as she walked, not bothering to look at Tender as she walked out into the cool spring air.

Tavera liked the town, at least for now. It was small and easy to deal with and the food at the bar was good. But she'd been here less than a phase and already people knew her. It made her nervous. She liked Tender too. His eyes were a bit sticky, as they said, and they were stuck on Tavera. But he was kind and honest and wanted to help people. People could use helping, Tavera knew that. She wasn't sure she wanted the kind of guidance Tender wanted to give her, but it was a nice change of pace, to see someone come to the aid of another. Care for them. Love them.

Tavera stopped in her tracks. The man named Little stood behind a tree, watching her. Tavera narrowed her eyes and frowned, pulling her shawl around her more tightly.

"Little, right?" she called. "What, did your brother send you after me too?"

Tavera wasn't sure if he was nervous about having been caught or if he sincerely thought if he said nothing, she'd move on. For a few breaths he remained behind the tree, but must have realized Tavera wasn't going anywhere; he stepped out onto the path. Tavera looked him up and down again, noting his gear. "No, you must have spotted me coming back from the forest," she said. "Wanted to check me out again for yourself. Catch anything?"

"No," Little said. He gave her a sidelong glance. His hair was too short in some places and too long in others. It stuck up in a way which made Tavera want to laugh. He seemed to have trouble looking her in the eye as well.

"You headed to service?" she asked. "It's starting in a little bit. I'm sure you'll hear your brother ring the bell."

"I ain't," Little said. There was a hint of defiance in his voice. It surprised Tavera, almost amused her.

"Of course you're not," Tavera said. "Because you're... getting a haircut instead?" He blushed and his ears did turn red, as Tavera had expected. She tittered. "No, that's not the reason. You don't like vespers?" she asked. "Prefer morning prayers?" She watched as he looked down at the ground, seeming self-conscious. "Afternoon? Don't like praying in a bar? Don't like the priestess? Your brother? Meeting a lady for some plowing?" Now he looked up, blushing even redder than before. Tavera laughed out loud.

"It's my business," he muttered, looking toward the forest. Tavera's eyes drifted toward the trees as well before they narrowed, frowning again.

"Oh, like me walking down this path is my own business?" she chided. "Is anyone's business their own? In a town this small?" Tavera made a sound in her throat and kept on walking. "Have your forest, Little Tender, and un-mind my business while you're at it. You and your brother. Allow a body to have some secrets."

"Everyone always has secrets," Little called after her. Tavera turned and grinned at him, walking backwards down the road.

"It's one of the lessons from the Goddess," she called, watching his face darken as she said it. She waved a hand at him before she turned and continued down the road. The spring air was cooling quickly and the weight of the shawl felt good around her shoulders. Tavera pulled it over her head as she walked through the town, wondering what secrets lay behind the unlocked doors of the homes and shops of Whitend. She doubted she would ever find them all. The secrets of other towns and other people would probably pull her out of this one long before she did.

Chapter 4
Prayers and Aid

Blessed Goddess
Holy Mother
Help your children
Love each other
Guide us with your gracious handful
Help us all to understand
Though the world
Around us rages
You are with us
Through the ages
Guide us with your grace each day
Holy Mam, these words we pray

Tender played the end of the closing song, the congregation lowing their hands from over their hearts. The scent of incense mixed with the evening air pouring in through the windows and the aroma of food cooking in the kitchen made Tavera's stomach gurgle. Sister Kella nodded to the people in the bar, holding her hands out to give the closing blessing.

"In Her waxing power, may you prosper, in Her growing light, may Her revelation shine. Go in mercy, love and peace. May Her Black Hand guide us."

"May Her Black Hand guide us," Tavera repeated, her voice joining the voices of the others. The closing words said, Tavera turned, the sound of chairs scraping against the floor telling her people were wasting no time in getting the room put back together for the evening. There were still a few hours of drinking, eating and gaming to be done. Tavera watched Tender put his hand on the priestess' shoulder and squeeze it warmly. He looked happy. Sister Kella looked tired. The service over, he ducked into the kitchen to tend to the evening meal while the sister sat at the bar, with her elbows propped up on the bar top.

"Admirable sermon, Sister," Tavera said, slipping onto the seat beside her. Sister Kella looked at her, a bit of surprise on her face. "The Moonflower's Promise."

"Yes well, I've heard it often enough," Sister Kella said. She half huffed it. Tavera sensed the priestess was impatient, her eyes trailing towards the kitchen. "Where is that man with my spirits?"

As if summoned, Tender emerged from the back with a smile on his face. He no longer held his guitar but instead had a long clay pitcher, something written on it with purple wax. "Heartberry wine, spiced in the style of the year you came here. Brewed by my own hand."

"Your wine's always spicier than your mother's, but I like it." Sister Kella inspected the bottle, running her thumb over the seal.

"Her beers are older, more subdued but better blended," Tender admitted.

"Age will do that, to beer at least," Kella chortled, tucking the bottle under her arm. "A good woman your mother was. In the Goddess' Bosom, to be sure." Kella slipped down from the stool and nodded to Tender, bowing her head to Tavera. "Put it on my tab, Tender. And good evening to you both."

Tavera watched as the priestess left the bar, then looked back to Tender. There was a sadness in his expression that made Tavera feel sad too, made her wonder about the priestess with the bloodshot eyes and hidden flask. Before Tavera could think of something comforting to say, Tender spoke up.

"You ever want to help someone, but you can't?" he asked. His question struck her in the chest, squeezing her heart. She thought of Derk and her promise to him, walking to the city gate and out of the town before she could change her mind, before she could turn back. Waiting outside Gam's place for too long before leaving the west Valley and coming here. Without even asking her if she wanted it, Tender poured her a drink. She took a sip while she considered her words.

"Everyone's been in that situation," was all she said. There was truth in that.

"I just --" Tender cut himself short. He sighed and poured himself a drink too, the liquid sloshing in the mug. "I don't know what to do. I know something's wrong. I just don't know what."

"She's been here what, seven years? If you haven't figured it out and she ain't told you…" Tavera just shrugged. "Maybe it's not meant for you to know."

"Six years, six and a half," Tender said. "I just…she's been here so long. When she first turned up, I didn't mind as much. She wasn't as bad. But over the years, she's grown worse and now with us being out of the Barony…" His voice trailed off again.

"Do you want her to get better for her own sake or for your own?" Tavera asked, trying to keep the disdain out of her voice. She must have failed. Tender's eyes shot up, his face coloring with embarrassment.

"For her own, of course!" Tender said. "It's sad to see a soul so pressed upon. So sad. When there are people around who would like to help."

"Maybe she thinks she's helping you by keeping it to herself. Maybe she's helping herself by keeping it tucked away," Tavera tried to reason. "Or maybe…maybe she's not ready to be helped." Tavera looked down into her cup. "You can't force someone, if they're not ready."

"Maybe she doesn't realize she needs help," Tender said. The way he said it, Tavera thought maybe he meant it as much for her as he did for Kella.

"Or perhaps," she added, draining her glass before she set it down on the bartop, smacking her lips before she spoke. "she knows you're not the one to set her right." Tender looked hurt. His mouth pulled to the side as he looked away from her. "Look, we can sit here all night talking maybes, or you can go to her home, take her alcohol, lock her up and get her on the mend. What're you going to do, Tender?"

"What would you do?" he asked. He seemed genuinely curious.

"I'd let her have her drink," Tavera said. "It's what she wants. For reasons she don't want to give. Help her when she asks." Tavera thought back to when she was little and Derk had taken her on. He had helped her in a way, without asking, hadn't he? If he had asked her to leave Prisca, to join him on his tramps through the Valley, to learn how to fight and steal because she'd be good at it, what would she have said? Tavera couldn't say. She had been a little girl then. Quiet and prone to crying. What would Tavera want, if she was in the priestess' cloak? If someone tried to comfort her about Derk, she'd probably laugh it off and change the subject. He was her pa, and her memories of him were hers alone.

"Do you think she will ask, when she needs it?" Tender asked.

"If you're still there for her, yeah," Tavera said. She smirked at him and put a coin on the counter. "You worry too much, Braxton Tender," she said. "You really do."

"It's only because I care," Tender said. She should have laughed at him when he said it but instead she just nodded and smiled.

"You're one of the good ones, aren't you?" she asked, knowing the answer already. Tender grinned at her in response, wagging his eyebrows at her.

"Can't we all be good ones?" he responded, taking the cork off the bottle again.

"No," Tavera sighed, smiling all the same. "Not really." She slipped off the chair and turned to head out, knowing Tender would call for her.

"Where're you off to now?" he asked. "I was going to give you a drink, on the house."

"I ran into Black Cera when I was out walking earlier and she invited me over for a game of cards after service," Tavera said. "I've already kept her waiting so I'd best be off."

"Not even for a free drink? With good company?" he asked. Tender shook the bottle.

"Don't worry, I'm sure Cera will have plenty to drink at hers," Tavera replied, grinning. "Besides, you have customers to see to and talk to, right? You spend too much time talking to me, Tender. Tend to your customers."

"Alright, have your game," Tender said.

"So nice of you to allow it," Tavera quipped. "Don't go and do anything rash while I have my bets," she chided, wagging a finger at him.

"I'll see what I can do, Miss Point," Tender said, smiling. "I'll give you that free drink tomorrow."

Tavera cocked her head to the side. "Who says I'll be here tomorrow?" She watched his brows knit on his forehead. "I'm going to win some money tonight and hit the road. I'll be in Ayilkin proper well before supper, even if I have a nap for midday meal."

"Tomorrow?" Tender said. It was almost a squeak.

"Yeah, know anyone heading into the Barony tomorrow? I'll walk if I have to, but a ride is always nice."

"I...don't think so," Tender said. He seemed less interested in the drink now, his eyes set on the bar top.

"Ah, well, a long walk it is." Tavera smirked, and turned and left the bar, walking past a couple entering. She pulled her hood up and looked around, trying to remember how to get to Black Cera's house. A few lamps lit the streets, illuminating the packed dirt roads of the town. Tavera found the street she was supposed to take and started down. Dark clouds wafted across the sky, a crescent moon shining beyond their reach. Tavera sniffed the air. It smelled like rain. She pulled her jacket about her more tightly and walked on, pushing thoughts of Tender from her mind and wondering what she would win at cards tonight.

Chapter 5
The Stranger

Tavera opened the door to her room and stopped. She wanted to laugh but she didn't. Instead she walked inside, closing the door behind her. Tavera could still feel the effects of Cera's home-brewed spirits but she could tell when someone was in her room. It was sad, really. "I'm surprised it took you this long to sneak into my room." she said loudly.

The room was dark but the faint light of a moon which was somewhere between a crescent and a half licked at the edges of the man sitting on her bed. He moved, falling into the light so Tavera could see the visage of the nosy barkeep, surprise still playing under his mustache. He brushed his hair back before he shrugged. Even in the dark she saw the gesture. "Well, no need to drag it out. Are you leaving?"

"Yes, I am," she said, sitting on the bed next to him and nudging him hard with her shoulder as she unbuckled her boots. He scooted over a bit as she kicked off one boot and then the other. "My game went well. I'm thinking I should get myself to a place I can spend my winnings. Nothing here I really want to spend them on." Tavera turned her face upward, locking onto Tender. "What're you still doing here?"

Her words made the barkeep stand up finally. He seemed uncomfortable in the dark, looking around and taking a few steps so his back was against the wall. She couldn't help but half snort, half laugh as he bumped into something, the sound of metal and leather clattering to the floor. Tavera knelt down, picking up the shortsword, bringing it as close to Tender as she could without it touching him, leaning it up against the stool again. The man squirmed slightly and Tavera found a smirk remaining on her lips as she started to remove her belt.

"Where'd you get that sword?" he asked, his voice seeming less steady. Tavera threw her belt to the side, the buckle hitting something before it fell to the floor.

"What are you doing in my room?" she asked, deliberately keeping her voice low and calm to contrast his. Thin fingers began to pull at the cords of her underbust, loosening the article of clothing. The thin, taut fabric fell away, her shirt billowing slightly freed from the restrictive garment. A few items she had hidden in her bodice fell to the ground as well, bouncing and scattering as they struck the wooden floor. Tavera cursed, kneeling to pick them up, Tender doing the same. She heard him grunt as some part of him hit the side of the bed

"Is it your room now? Have you grown attached to it?" Tender handed something to her; the cool, thin shape of it told her it was a pin. Tavera threaded it into the abandoned bodice, tilting her head to the side as she faced Tender.

"Not attached, no. I'll be able to leave it easy enough." Tavera quickly undid the buttons of her skirts, slipping them off before laying the thick garment on top of the bodice. She stood there in her shift, feeling chilled but resisting the urge to shiver. "I don't stay in any one place too long," she continued. "I move about. It's my way." She put her hands on his broad shoulders, turning him around, pointing him toward the door. "The door's that way. Don't slam it, I expect they've all fallen back asleep by now."

"Now wait a minute," Tender hissed, wheeling around. The moonlight coming through the window played off the lines of his face as he stood before her. Tavera crossed her arms over her chest and stuck her chin out, waiting for whatever it was he had to say. "I asked you a question," Tender said, more calmly. "This is my tavern. I have a responsibility to my patrons as a business owner and to the people of this town as their leader. Now tell me, Miss Point," he said. He paused. For a moment she thought maybe he would drop the question but instead he just looked sad. "Why do you have a sword?"

Her mouth went dry as the words registered. Why was he asking? Dark eyes searched his face and all she saw there was earnestness and concern. He didn't ask in a malicious or even an accusatory way. For a moment she thought of Lori, who was not supposed to be on watch when the heist had gone down. There was something in Tender's face which reminded her of him. She turned her face away, tears glimmering briefly in her eyes. As quickly as the thoughts had sprung up, she squashed them. Tavera kept her voice steady as she answered him.

"I have the sword for the same reason most people have them. To stab people. Or at least make them think I'll stab them. And as I'm leaving in the morning, you won't have to worry about the safety of your patrons much longer. I doubt I'll hack them to pieces between now and morning."

"Where'd you get it?"

"It was a gift from a madman. At least that's what I've heard of the man who gave it to me."

"And can you use it?" Now Tender's voice was quiet. She felt like Tender knew the answer and didn't want to hear it but asked all the same.

"I wouldn't carry a sword if I didn't know how to use it," Tavera said.

There was a moment of silence in the room. A chill wind began to blow through the open window and Tavera stepped quietly toward it, closing it and drawing the latch to lock it. For a breath she thought Tender would leave the room but instead he just stood there. She heard him breathing, could almost hear him thinking.

"Will you go for a walk with me?" Tender asked at last.

Tavera looked to the side, not sure what to say. She was tired after a night of gambling and drinking; but after tomorrow she would probably never see Tender again, not unless she wanted to. Tavera finally nodded and pulled her skirts back on, not bothering to slip on her bodice. Instead she just smirked when Tender held her cloak out to her and took it, draping it about her shoulders. He held the door open for her, following her down the stairs and unlocking the door to the tavern before they stepped out into the night.

It was still cold outside, the breeze biting through her cloak and sleeves. Tavera shivered slightly, hugging herself with her arms. Tender didn't seem to be bothered by the cold night air. The village was quiet. Only a few windows were yellow with light, most of the people having turned in long ago. The farmhouse she had been gambling at was now just another black shape against a black sky, the ornery farmers probably going to bed not too long after she had left. Her thoughts strayed to what Tender wanted to talk about on the walk. Was this about her gambling? The weapon?

"Tender has not always been our family name," he started, his deep voice clear, his tone implying he was beginning a story. They continued for another few paces before he began again. "Our family name back in the old country of Haran used to be Baya, which means 'Way Seeker.' I come from a long line of caravan leaders, trail blazers and sky readers. Our family was in the business of helping people through wild places, back when all families were back east, in Holy Haran."

"How do you know this?" Tavera asked. It wasn't entirely common for families in the Valley to be able to trace back their Haranian roots, with good reason. Many of the families who came to the Valley had suffered in Haran, wishing to put the abuse and terror behind them as they settled into the Valley. Many had chosen new family names upon their arrival, or so the priestesses said in their sermons.

"My mam told me all this," Tender said. A proud smile crossed his face, his eyes shining with nostalgia. "Ever since I was a little boy, she told me stories of our family beginnings, especially because us Tenders were so few at that point. Just me, her and Little." He paused and the bit of happiness Tavera had seen faded slightly. He sighed. "In the region of Haran they came from, the family was well known. They were employed by wealthy nobles, able to find and secure safe, fast ways to get their goods from one territory to the next. The family worked together, forming a business of sorts, one part of the family taking one area, one part taking another, passing everything along," he said.

"Then, the war happened," he continued. "The land began to separate, not physically, but...morally, idealistically." Tender paused and looked towards his bar, the temple for the town. "It started in the pulpits and trickled down to the pews before spilling out onto the streets. People began to fight, using what they believed in their hearts as fuel to put their hands to violence. Old agreements went unhonored, contracts were burned and the repercussions physical. Houses no longer dealt with one another at best. Families began to come apart. My family was not spared from the in-fighting. They took sides. The only blood that mattered was that which was spilled.

"However, my great-grandfather refused to take up arms. He tried to win people over with sense, asking how they could kill people they had been allies with just a season ago. He did not condemn the changes taking place but he publicly renounced the methods people were using to achieve it. People threatened him and his family. They set fire to his home, to his stores, destroyed his livelihood." Tender winced and Tavera frowned in sympathy. "Yet he refused to draw a sword against someone just because their ideas were different and he would not kill someone in a religious fervor."

They stopped in front of a fence, Tender leaning against the split rails. Tavera stood opposite him, wondering about Tender's ancestors and their own steadfast natures. "When the conflicts died down," Tender started up again, "and the resolutions had been made, as we know, there were still those who were unhappy with the results. Our people, those who would come to live in the Valley, felt betrayed by their country and left. My great-grandfather was ostracized for not picking a side, for not killing people's sons and daughters in the fray. He found himself disillusioned and when the Separatists left, he went with them, taking his daughter and wife with him. But not before garnering the nickname, 'Tender,' since the people believed he did not pick a side out of weakness and not because of the strength of his convictions. He wore it with pride and when his son was born, he gave it to him as his surname, as well as changing the name of his daughter to match when they did the Valley census."

Tavera could only nod as Tender told the story, his voice low and nostalgic as he told the tale. She had heard about the origins of the people of Ten Crescents, how they had come to escape religious persecution, to start anew after years of fighting in a faraway land called Haran. The stories of the great leaders were told on every Founders' Day, about how they traveled for weeks and dealt with harsh terrain and harsh weather and creatures, all to escape oppression, and how they found this valley after a huge earthquake, the crescent lakes showing that the Lunar Goddess had indeed set this place aside for them.

But she had never heard anyone speak of their family specifically, never heard an actual name inserted into the stream of events, save the great leaders of the Seperatists on Founder's Day. As the story unfolded, Tender seemed to stand up taller, grow bigger, the same tranquility that she had noticed on his face during the fight lying on his features. He looked as if he was the hero in the story he'd just told.

Tender stopped walking, turning to face Tavera. The night was still except for the sound of a horse snorting. Tavera tilted her head up slightly, looking into his eyes. The man was smiling, his eyes warm as he looked at her. "Do you know why I am telling you this, Miss Point?"

"I don't, to be honest," Tavera said.

"I am telling you this because I don't want you to leave thinking that I am a fool," Tender said. "I wanted to explain why I am the way I am. It's in my blood to help people and I don't mind doing it. The Tenders have a history of sticking by what they believe in and what they believe is to do what is right. Now I know you aren't out and out bad. I've seen you talking to people around town, helping some children with their games and such. But I also saw you at the temple meeting and you looked so distressed."

Tavera turned her face away from Tender. She could tell he wanted to put his hand on her cheek or her shoulder, to comfort her with a touch, but he didn't. "You're too pretty to look so sad. Tell me…what is wrong?"

Tavera wanted to smack him away. She didn't want to answer. Tears pricked at the corners of her eyes. Thoughts of Derk had sprung up during the sermon. Kella had spoken of the moonflower growing best on disturbed earth, dirt which had been upturned, and how it grew best on graves. Out of death and turmoil, the beauty of the flower proliferated. Her father's capture and Lori certainly made Tavera feel like upturned earth, strange hands digging into her and turning her around.

Could something beautiful bloom from her life in the state it was in? Where would the seeds come from? Sitting before Kella, Tavera had come to grips with the fact her life had never really been smooth planting, had it? But with Derk she had had some stability. Company. Love. Now what did she have? The Cup, possibly, if she could find them. And this Tender, standing before her, waiting for an answer as to why she was so sad.

Before she could say anything, she heard a door slam open, light from within throwing an orange glow before the doorway. Two figures stepped out of a house, the first one stumbling over the threshold as if pushed. Tavera narrowed her eyes, trying to see who was being thrown out of their home, her heart thumping as she realized it was Kella, the priestess. From where Tavera stood she saw the priestess' face was stricken with fear. The sister's eyes went wide as they fell upon her and Tender. "Tender!" she called out, panic in her voice. "Help me!"

"Kella!" Tender shouted, running toward the small house. Tavera ran after him, stopping just a few paces away from where Kella stood. Whoever had pushed the priestess out of her own home emerged from behind Kella, standing alongside her. He grabbed her by the hair. Kella's head jerked back sharply as he brought a small sickle to her neck. The long, thin shine of the blade glinted in the scant light of the evening.

The man was of an average height with brushed-back reddish hair. His skin was pale, almost deathly so and though his face was not old, it was worn by weather and bad living. Tavera cringed at the main feature of his face. His left eye, plucked out long ago was the focal point of a long, crescent-shaped scar running from his forehead, over his eye and under his nose. It gave his face a wicked appearance. The strange man snarled as he pressed the knife to the priestess' throat, pulling her with him as he took a step back.

"Take one step closer," he hissed, his voice sending shivers down Tavera's back, "and I will paint her dress red, do you understand me?"

Tavera's eyes darted to the side, looking to the horse and then through the open doorway. He had obviously come a long way. She glimpsed a table with a pitcher on it, one mug on the floor, a chair on its side as if it had been knocked over. Tavera scanned the priestess' face and found a hint of shame trying to hide behind her fear.

"I don't think you will," Tavera said, holding her hands up and not daring to take a step closer. She saw Tender looking at her out of the corner of her eye but she fixed her gaze on the strange, ugly man, tilting her chin toward him. "I know you don't want to hurt her and you don't have to. Let's just all --"

"How DARE YOU!" came the loud, booming voice of the barkeep, the shock of his words almost making Tavera take a step back. Obviously he didn't think they should talk. Tender panted, his eyes shimmering with rage as they focused on the thin man before them. "You have the gall to threaten the PRIESTESS of this community?" His hands were balled into fists, his eyes dead-set and cold as he glared at the stranger. "Sir, you will unhand her or I will thrash you for daring to do such a thing!"

"I will not unhand her," the man shouted. He pushed the priestess to the ground, the older woman screaming. As soon as she was out of his way, Tender rushed the man, fists raised to do battle.

Tender swung, a powerful blow which should have sent the man to the ground. The stranger was unmoved. The impact of the blow did nothing but shock the barkeep in its inability to hurt him. "Tits," Tender cursed, as the strange man focused his eyes on the barkeep. Tavera's heart pumped in her chest. She knelt, drawing her dagger from her boot, looking to where Kella lay on the ground. The priestess sobbed, her body rocking up and down, her face hidden. Tavera wrapped her fingers around the hilt of the dagger and looked back to Tender and the man. The man's gloved fist struck Tender squarely across the jaw, sending him reeling. The stranger then sent a booted foot squarely into Tender's gut, doubling him over.

The barkeep lay moaning to the ground, clutching his stomach. While Tavera wanted to make sure Tender was alright, now was her chance. It was the only way she could help Tender and the priestess now, the strange man focused on the barkeep. Tavera threw the dagger, the piece of sharp metal aimed for the man's stomach. But as the metal blade slipped from her fingers, the stranger pointed his crescent-shaped knife at her, a cruel grin on his terrible face.

Everything seemed to slow down. Red sparkles glowed on the edge of the sickle, came off the blade and floated to her. Sound, time and vision muffled and crawled as the lights settled around her head and turned white. Her eyes burned as the world became a painful, searing illumination before her. If Tavera screamed in pain, she didn't hear it. Eventually everything around her faded back to red. Then the world turned black, her limbs losing their strength as she slumped blindly to the ground.

Chapter 6
Dark Corners

A candle flickered in the corner of the room, its yellow and orange light creeping across the blackness. The only sound was a faint dripping noise from above. The floor below her was scratchy and coming apart. Tavera sniffed and felt around, trying to figure out what it was. It wasn't the floor at all. It was hay. She was lying in a pile of hay. The room seemed familiar, though she thought it should have been bigger for some reason. Now the space seemed too small, almost suffocating.

From the darkness beyond the candlelight, a figure stepped up. Tavera gasped, all of her words stuck in her throat. Tears sprang to her eyes as he walked into the light and up to her, staring down.

"How could you do it, Tavera?" Derk's voice made the tears finally fall but his tone kept her from speaking still. He looked terrible. His blond hair was dirty, his face haggard, his skin dry. His clothes, torn and muddy, hung off his gaunt frame. He stroked his scruffy beard, gray and yellow, his blue eyes unnaturally bright in the dark. "How could you leave me there?"

Tavera blinked, tears still streaming down her face. She looked down at her hands. They were tied at the wrists. She stared at the carefully knotted ropes before gazing up into her pa's face again. Her mouth opened and closed a few times before she could manage to make words. "How... but...Derk, you told me--"

"I know what I told you!" he shouted. It sounded so loud in the small room, Tavera winced. Derk bent forward and grabbed her by the throat, Tavera too shocked to cry out as he slammed her into the wall. "I told you that as your teacher. As my student you did the right thing. But you called me 'Pa' for all those years and when I got into trouble, you RAN away!" He slammed her into the wall again, and this time she did cry out, all her attempts to get away point- less. He had all of his weight on her and she tried to push him off, crying out in fear.

How had he gotten out? How had she gotten here? Why he was doing this? Her father dropped her to the floor and she landed on her side, unable to catch herself on her bound hands. A sharp pain shot through her wrist and Tavera cried out again. Derk chuckled in the orange glow.

"I, I wanted to help you, I did!" Tavera managed to sob. Surely he had to believe that, surely he knew. "I, I went back to where the man who had done the ceremony, where he was staying, but he was gone! I really looked and then someone from the Cup told me I had to leave, they were looking for me! I even went to Portsmouth, to see if I couldn't get Gam to help me, but she never showed!" The tears in her eyes made the room blurry and she felt snot running from her nose. "I waited three days! I heard browncloaks all over the west side were cracking down, putting people in jail! And I didn't know what to do. So...so I did what you had told me to do." Why hadn't she tried harder to get him out? What more could she have done? "I'm...I'm on my way to Tyeskin, to see if I can't find Lights. Maybe he can help."

"Lights? That fapper? Are you going there to help me or help yourself?" Derk sneered. "You aren't trying now, are you? Couldn't even throw a brick when I got caught. You just froze, didn't you? Walked out?"

Tavera suddenly felt inadequate and stupid. Worst of all, she felt like she had failed Derk, the only person who had ever loved her and the only parent she had ever really known. It was horrible. She thought she had cried all the tears she could have over this but her heart felt as if it would rip in her chest and she sobbed in pain and grief.

"I thought…I did…what you wanted me to do," Tavera cried. "It was hard to do it, Pa, it was."

"Not as hard as sitting in jail. I know what you did. You betrayed me."

"What?" Tears froze in her eyes as his words hit her brain, the audacity of the accusation cutting through her emotions. Tavera blinked, trying to wipe her eyes with her hands. She winced as she got hay in them, the shards of dry grass scratching. She tried to brush the hay out, the sharp pain growing as she furtively tried to clear it.

"You heard me," came the voice. This time, Derk stood very close. Before she could do anything, she was on her feet, her back pressed up against the wall again. The pressure across her shoulders felt as if he would break her collarbones. "I think you turned me in, to be rid of me." "No, it isn't true, it could never be true," she gasped, tears and snot catching in her throat. Somewhere in the wobbling, watery light which was the world there came a flash of something metal. Then the cool, sharp sensation of a knife to her throat. Still, her eyes could not focus and Tavera tried not to cry. Couldn't he see he was hurting her? "Stop, Derk, please, you're hurting me! I'm sorry!"

Her eyes burned. A single candle burned somewhere in the background. The darkness seemed more inviting and Tavera wished for it, wanting nothing more than to be back in the stupefying darkness of ignorance. Derk pushed her down to her knees, scraping her skin and rattling her bones. She felt him move behind her, grabbing her roughly by the hair and jerking her head back. The knife moved up to where her head met her neck.

"I don't care about that. I gave you your life and you threw mine away. I hate you, Tavera. I hate you and no one will ever care about you ever again. Especially not when I'm through with you."

Panic welled up inside of her. Tavera shrieked, trying to pull away, yanking her hair from his grasp. She fell forward to the ground, pain shooting through her bound wrists. Before she could get up, he was on her, pinning her to the ground. Hay scraped at her eyes and her face was wet, tears streaming down her cheeks. His weight was as heavy as the guilt she felt about leaving him and the more she fought him, the more it hurt. No one could hear her, she was sure of that, but still, she tried to scream, tried to do something to stop her world from crushing her to death.

"No, Derk, NO!"

"She's awake! Quick, hold her down!"

"Hold her down!"

"I'm trying! OW!"

Tavera's hands could finally move. The first thing she did was strike out with a fist, her knuckles bashing into something. She heard someone stumbling back, booted feet on a wooden floor. Tavera tried to open her eyes but they wouldn't cooperate. They were stuck closed. "Get OFF of me," she shouted. Tavera struck out again, pushing off the weight of whoever was on her with a grunt. Tavera caught someone under their chin with her elbow and sat up. When she was sure no one was touching her or near her, she pried open her crusted eyes with her fingers.

The room came into focus slowly, the crust on her eyes flaking onto her cheeks, collecting in her lashes. Her eyes still hurt as they had in...her dream. It must have been a dream. When she rubbed at her eyes she felt something dry scrape against her skin. Her hands were covered with large, crusty brown flakes of dried blood. Tavera looked up, still shaking from what had just happened, her head jerking around as she looked about the room.

"How did I get here?" she demanded, her voice quavering slightly. One of the people in the room started as she spoke. She was back in the room Tender had given her, in the bed she had never slept in last night. The sun coming in through the window told her it was well into the morning. Three villagers she didn't recognize just stared at each other. One of them, a tall, lanky farmer looked to someone who may have been his son and pointed toward the door with his chin, the boy staring at Tavera with wide eyes. He ran out the door, his footsteps loud and clunky down the stairs.

"Miss...Point, is it?" the farmer asked. "We...we brought you here, after we found you. You and Tender got into a skirmish with a stranger who escaped on horseback." The farmer blinked his watery blue eyes. "Don't you remember?"

The fight...the...stranger with the scar. A woman held out a damp towel to her and she snatched it, not able to keep from glaring at her as she took it. Tavera wiped her eyes, seeing the red-and-rust-colored blood. The stranger had knocked Tender out and then he had...he'd pointed that sickle at her. There had been lights and then darkness and then the dream.

Had it been a dream? A sickness crept into the pit of her stomach as she recalled it. It couldn't have just been a dream. It had felt so real, both physically and emotionally. Tavera felt the guilt and the knife and the hands, heard Derk's cruel words. Tavera shuddered. Something about it had been real, though obviously some of it had been a dream. It had been in the little room under the bar, where Derk had first taken her all those years ago. She had been scared then too, but not like this. The guilt and the pain had felt worse than anything else she had experienced before, even worse than the initial shock over losing her father in the first place. Could her father have done that to her? How could she even imagine it? It was horrific.

The sound of loud footsteps approached and broke the tension in the room as Tender, the boy and Little walked into the room. Tender's face was ashen, his eyes wide with concern. He seemed startled by her and he looked to the boy. "A drink for her, get to it," he barked. "All of you clear out," he said to the rest of them. "Give her some space." The farmer and the girl left the room, leaving Tavera there with Tender and Little

"Thank the Goddess you're alright, Miss Point," Tender said, taking a step toward her. She gave him a look which stopped him in his tracks and he stepped back. His face was badly bruised where the stranger had punched him. It gave his face a crooked kind of look to it, his hair mussed and his shirt open to the chest. "I'm…I'm sorry. We were very worried. No one in the community knew what he had done to you. The symptoms were troubling and…no one could rouse you." Tender took a deep breath. "We thought he had put a death-sleep on you."

"If only," was all she said, standing up from the bed, not surprised to find her legs unsteady beneath her. Tender lunged forward to help her, and she allowed him, fighting the urge to recoil as he touched her. It had only been a dream, after all. The pain in her eyes reminded her of the hay from her dream and her stomach knotted and turned with the recent memory.

"Are you alright?" Tender asked. Again, concern played on his bruised face. She could see him trying not to wince as he spoke. Tavera nodded, sighing heavily as she found her balance, the men taking their hands off her, much to her relief. Little smiled sheepishly at her before returning his gaze to the floor.

"Why the twixt did you bring him here?" she asked, her voice croaking as she spoke. Tavera began rummaging through her bag for some food, hoping it would settle her stomach. "You think a sick body wants a strange one near?"

"I had him come to help." Tavera looked over Little, frowning slightly as she continued to search through her bag without looking. With the two of them before her, the lack of resemblance was uncanny. Tender had dark hair that hinted at having been lighter when he was younger, and dark eyes. While he definitely wasn't fat, he was well-muscled. That coupled with his undying confidence made the barkeep a formidable figure in any setting. Little was sinewy, his arms looking like they were made from thick, strong vines, the veins popping out as if his skin was on too tight. His hair was sticking up more than usual today and his eyes were light and hadn't connected with anyone since he had walked through the door. He didn't look as if he would be helping with anything besides making himself feel more uncomfortable and Tavera snorted quietly, finally finding an old biscuit in her pack.

"The villagers heard the shouts and came to the scene after we were both...dealt with," Tender continued. "The man told them he was taking the priestess hostage unless…." Tender trailed off for a breath, wincing when he frowned. "Unless we delivered something they think she has to them in a few days' time. I thought maybe Little could help us with that."

"Well…" she said, taking a bite out of the biscuit and walking right up to Little, standing too close to him on purpose. She chewed loudly as she stared into his face, the young man obviously trying very hard not to seem nervous but failing miserably. She was glad he felt nervous. Better him than her. She swallowed half of what was in her mouth before speaking. "What can he do, exactly?"

"He…he's a tracker. He can help us find the stranger." Tender took his brother's arm and pulled him out of her cold gaze, giving the girl a curious look. "You're obviously still out of sorts, Miss Point so we'll leave you to rest--"

"No!" Tavera shouted, not meaning to, her expression going from cold to troubled in a breath. Her mouth opened as she thought of what she wanted to say, not wanting to reveal what she felt. She definitely did not want to rest and she most certainly did not want to be alone with her thoughts. Tavera hoped they did not notice her hands shook as she grabbed her cloak, draping it over her shoulders so she wouldn't have to bother with fastening it. "Have you…have you found this thing the stranger was looking for?"

"No," Tender replied. "We've mostly been waiting for you to wake up, getting patched up."

"I haven't been getting patched up," Little muttered, the first words he had spoken since he had entered the room. Tavera smiled at the look Tender gave him. She pushed past the both of them, leaving her room and trying to leave the thoughts of her dream behind her.

"We should go to the priestess' place. There is something I would like to see, I think it will help us…find her."

Chapter 7
Broken Truths

Before Tender could protest, she was out the door. Her boots clunked down the stairs and across the floor as she exited, ignoring the people who stared. She heard Tender and Little following after her and Little muttering to himself. Spring clouds billowed above and the air smelled chilled and green. Tavera locked eyes on the house in question and half jogged there, Tender finally running up to her side. "How long was I out?" she asked.

"A few hours. It's almost time for morning meal," he said. They both slowed as they approached the house. Tavera looked around the small patch of packed dirt, her hands on her hips as she surveyed the area.

"No one found a dagger, did they?" she asked. She had thrown it. It wasn't on the ground. Tender shook his head; his brother stared up at the sky.

"No; a few people said they got here as you fell. The stranger told them to bring the Goddess Plate by the eclipse or he would kill the priestess. Then he pointed at the house and all of the roofs were on fire, white and hot. By the time they had alerted the town, he was gone and the fire just... disappeared."

"Nothing was damaged?" she asked.

"Nothing, not a single scorch mark or piece of charcoal." Tender walked to where the stranger's horse had been tied up, looking at the ground. "It was a wielding of some sort. The priestess was knocked out and laid across the front of the horse."

Tavera nodded, pondering Tender's words as she pushed open the door to the house. Inside, the fire in the hearth had burned out but morning light came through the windows, giving her more than enough light to work by. She stepped in, surveying the room and recalling what she had seen yesterday, trying to piece it together.

"She knew him," Tavera said, taking another step. Being in someone else's house always put her in good spirits, especially when she knew she hadn't been invited. The fact she was there to help didn't change that. Tavera stepped aside and out of the doorway so Tender could walk in as well.

"How could Kella know him?" he asked. She saw he was looking at her out of the corner of her eye but still, she remained focused on the task, walking around the table and ignoring Tender's disbelief. "I mean, I know she's not exactly a model of goodness but...I find it hard to believe. He was obviously a...a...."

"A bad man? The kind that might give her trouble?" A bottle of wine sat on the table, the top uncorked. Tavera picked it up and sniffed at it, swirling it around so its scent wafted up to her nose. "This...didn't you sell this to her last night?"

"I did," Tender said, his brows starting to furrow. The barkeep walked up to Tavera and took the bottle from her, looking at the few gulps left at the bottom and then to the table. The two glasses were still there, one of them over-turned. The spill still marked a dark spot on the wooden table and floor. "Obviously she bought it for them to share."

"Or they shared it, at least," she said. She took the bottle from his hands and without hesitation she gulped down the rest of it, setting it down on the table before she walked over to the low-lying bed. It was still made. Just drinks were shared. There was a small chest at the foot of the bed. Tavera began pulling up the sheets.

"What are you doing?" Tender said loudly, rushing over as Tavera picked up the mattress. He stopped short as Tavera pointed at something. A small, bound book, its leather worn and once a silvery gray, now just seeming dirty. He bent down and took the book.

Tavera let the mattress fall, brushing her hands on her lap. It had been filled with hay and the feeling made her skin crawl. She pushed it from her mind, turning her attention to the small trunk. It had a lock on it, though just from looking at it the thief knew it was more of an inconvenience than an actual challenge. Tavera dropped to her knees and pulled a pin out of her boot, not considering whether what she was about to do might seem strange. "What's in the book?"

"Pictures," Tender said. His back was to her and he flipped through the pages, the thick paper rustling. "Drawings. Some of people. Mostly of people." Tender set a chair upright so he could sit on it. "The later ones are of people from here. I'm in here--" The way his voice cut short suggested something was wrong. Tavera looked up and saw he blushed slightly. He stared at the picture for a while before he turned the next page. The lock on the trunk popped open right when it was supposed to.

"The man from yesterday, he's in here!" He almost knocked Tavera over as he crouched next to her, but she steadied herself with one hand. It was undeniably the stranger. He was younger, a smile on his too-thin mouth, but it was him. The illustration was on one of the first pages of the journal. Beside his picture, in careful yet shaky hand-writing was written, "The Leader of the Temple of the Red Moon Rising. Cy, the inquisitor, the twister of words, the render of hearts."

"What do you know about Sister Kella, Braxton?" Tavera kept her voice soft and low, a seriousness seeming to weigh heavily around them. Tender took in a deep breath, looking down at the face printed in black-and-red ink.

"She was sent here by her superiors a few years after my mother died," Tender began. "She was once a priestess at the Waning Crescent Temple, in Reedsend." He stopped.

Tavera shook her head. She knew there was more to it. Tender had spoken about wanting to help Kella. As the leader of the town and barkeep, he probably knew more about Kella than he let on, something he had hinted at when he had spoken with Tavera just last night. Tavera hadn't really listened, at least not about Kella. Tavera sighed. "What else, Tender?" she asked quietly. "Why did you want to help her?"

Tender looked down at the book, turning a page. "When she arrived here," he began, "she was already in a bad way, drinking often and too much. She always seemed...dis-traught. I would fetch her for prayers and she would be speaking nonsense." He stopped again, turning another page in the journal. "I wondered why they sent her here, in the state she was in. I'd find her talking about how they owed her and how they had used her. Kella never said who 'they' were." The barkeep's shoulders drooped, and he turned a few more pages in the book.

Tavera got up and stood beside Tender, looking over the entries. The portraits were interspersed with menacing landscapes and troubling scenes, dark pathways and staircases all leading off into the distance. One motif played throughout the journal: a crescent moon, sometimes in black, sometimes in red, off in the distance. Something about those pictures sent a chill down Tavera's spine. Tender closed the book.

"I think we're going to find that out ourselves." Tavera went back and crouched before the trunk, pushing it open. "What about this 'plate' you mentioned?"

"I have no idea," Tender said. "I mean, I'm guessing it's just a Goddess Plate like the ones they use in bigger temples, but we've never used one here. My mother didn't use them and Sister Kella kept our tradition." Tender scratched his head, mussing his hair "Obviously, he means a specific one. He seems to think she has it or knows something about it."

Tavera pawed through the items in the trunk. A few garments, robes, as well as a bottle of liquor, dark with age. A few bottles of ink threatened to ruin the contents of the trunk. Several blotchy stains suggested quite a few bottles of ink had accidentally opened inside. With a sigh, she pulled the garments out, throwing them onto the mattress.

"Braxton!" Heavy footsteps preceded Little's entrance. His blue eyes were big, his voice deep, probably one of the few things he shared with Tender. "Braxton, it's going to rain. It'll wash out the tracks if we don't go soon."

"It's alright, Little, we'll...I think we'll be on the road soon enough," Tender said. A folded sheet with embroidery at the edges covered whatever was at the bottom of the trunk. As Tavera lifted it her fingers ran against something sharp and cold, the pain in her fingers making her shout and draw her hand back with a start.

At the bottom of the trunk were more journals and piles of yellowed parchment. Gruesome pictures littered the bot-

tom in rusted red and muted black. Faces and alien landscapes stared up from the paper. Even more troubling than
the pictures was the crescent-shaped sickle. Its blade was
orangey-red with rust and disuse. Bright red blood drops
ran in a line across the papers, Tavera's blood a lively note
on the red-and-brown tarnish of the curved knife.

"What the twixt is this?" Tender demanded. Tavera
watched as he bent down, picking up the sickle in one hand
and one of the books in the other. The binding cracked as
he opened it, pages threatening to fall out. Tender turned
the pages, licking his lips as he looked them over. Little
stood up and peered over his shoulder, his watery blue eyes
wincing as they fell upon the page.

Tavera stood up finally, walking over to Tender's other
side to get a look. They were filled with more pictures but
this time, the illustrations included Kella. Tavera recognized
her face, creases under her eyes, eyes squeezed shut, dark
and empty. In some of the pictures she was lying in a corner somewhere, the word "forget" scrawled across the page
dozens of times. The face of the man called Cy showed up
with her. In some of the images his face was calm or laughing. Other times anger twisted his already frightening features. As the pages turned, the stranger's face came up more
often and the crescent watched from the corners of the
page, a smile on the kidnapper's face. The handwriting became more illegible, though the pictures became more
hopeful. Two figures were bright while the scene around
them was dark, both always in the same room, the stone
floor sketched with a meticulous hand, the texture of the
walls evident in the inks. Tender turned another page and
all three of them drew in their breaths.

Drawn across the center of the book, taking up two
pages was a horrific rendering of the Goddess. She held a

sickle in one hand, a humanoid figure in the other. The Goddess held the figure by the hair, back arched. A long, red slit had been painted down the middle of the person, from neck to belly, the red paint used to stain the page allowed to drip. Below the figure was a bowl where the blood collected. From the surface of its ghastly contents reached a disembodied arm. The Goddess seemed to be looking down at the arm, her face calm, unaffected by the grisly mass of flesh in her arms.

Tender tossed the book to the ground, the brittle pages snapping as they hit the floor. Something in the book caught Tavera's eye. She had to will herself to reach down and pick it up but she did, flipping through the yellowed pages.

Tucked between two of the pages, a short lock of red hair was lodged in the binding, whatever glue holding it there having lost its power long ago. In crisp-yet-wandering handwriting was written the simple phrase:

Please, help me to forget.

Something about the phrase was more chilling than the picture. Tavera snapped the book shut. The half-elf stared down at the journal in her hands, wondering what the priestess must have gone through and what her captors were now subjecting her to. She understood why the priestess drank and shirked her duties now. Though Tavera dreaded coming across the man named Cy again, she wished to help the priestess.

Tavera jumped as Tender threw the curved knife onto the table with a clatter. The barkeep ran his hands through his hair, breathing heavily as he paced in front of the table. In his frustration, he kicked the overturned wooden chair, cursing as the wood cracked and the piece of furniture went flying across the room. For a moment all three of them stood silent, Tavera and Little too scared to cut through Tender's emotions with their words and Tender breathing heavily, his eyes dark with anger.

"We're in over our heads!" he shouted, throwing a hand up in the air. He paced back and forth a few more times. "They, whoever they are, these cultists, they want us to get this plate and we have no idea what they are talking about, nor are we even sure of how to find them."

"I...I could maybe find them, Braxton," offered Little, his voice shaky.

"By the eclipse?! When is the eclipse?!"

"Um...six days, Braxton."

"Six days!" Tender shouted. "Six! After seeing all this...it looks like everything has come full circle for Kella, hasn't it?"

Tavera stood there for a moment, her mouth hanging open. She shook her head. "You're full of it." Her words were sharp and loud. Little stared at her. Tender just blinked at her, looking stupefied.

"You told me all you want to do is help people, give them their choices. You saw the sister. She was afraid and she was ashamed. She didn't want to go with him. She called out to you for help and now that her voice has trailed off, you won't answer her?" Tavera blinked and found an odd smile tugging at the corner of her mouth. "How dare you say she's getting hers because you're...you're scared."

"My brother isn't afraid of anything, Miss Point," Little said.

"Shut up, Herix!" Tender shouted. Tavera heard him breathing hard and she knew he was trying to think of the best way to say what he wanted to say. The man drew in his breath, his hands falling to his side helplessly. "I am scared," he said finally. "I am scared we won't be able to help her. I'm scared because it might already be too late to help her. I'm scared we might find her and wind up...I don't want to think about worst-case scenarios. I'm scared for the priestess and my brother who will invariably follow me." He gestured at Little, who was still blushing at being chastised, his eyes wandering around the room.

"Well, I'll help you keep an eye on him," Tavera said, watching Tender's eyes for surprise. It showed faintly through his hopelessness and he laughed slightly.

"I'm serious," Tavera said, her cheeks warming as she committed herself verbally to the party. "That bastard took my dagger with him and he did something to my head I didn't appreciate." She shrugged, looking down at the closed journal in her hand and thinking of the priestess who she now realized had been so distraught. "Besides, I've had many a priestess help me during my life and I'd like to return a favor."

Tender watched his brother meander off across the small room, sighing heavily as he shook his head. "I won't refuse your aid, though it would pain me to see something bad happen to you, Miss Point." The same look he had given her the first time they had met returned to his face and he smiled at her, a bit of joviality returning to the room.

"Don't worry about me," she offered, laughing gently. She started to gather up some of the drawings from the trunk and the journals; looking them over might offer up some clues. "I'm more than capable of looking after myself. Who knows? I might actually bail you out of a bad situation." She tried to keep her words light but in her mind, the reality of what she said weighed heavily on her. This was the real reason she wanted to go. Tavera worried Tender would miss something or offer mercy at the wrong time and get himself killed. That Tender should die trying to help another human being seemed so fitting. Yet Tavera vowed to do her damnedest to keep it from happening. He was too good of a person to die from a knife in the back. Tavera was used to knives in backs. Who better to shield Tender's than her?

"Well, no one is going to be in any situations if we don't find this plate," Tender said, picking up one of the glasses on the table and looking into it. "Not that I'm sure we'll find it. We don't know what we're looking for, and I'm not certain if we should give it to them." He walked over and took one of the pictures Tavera held, grimacing at the image. "Whatever they would use it for, it cannot be good."

"If we can find it, we should," Tavera said, tucking the papers into one of the journals. "If we find them and show up empty-handed, they might just take us prisoner. We'll need it as bait."

"But we have to get going soon, Little says it's going to rain and it'll make the going slower." Tender took the journal from Tavera and sat on the chair. "Maybe if we look over all of these, it will give us a clue as to the plate's whereabouts and where they might have taken her."

"Cy didn't just come here for a drink. He must think she knows and that we know. No point in telling us to bring it to him before the eclipse if he thought we couldn't." Tavera knelt down in front of the trunk, pulling out another journal and another pile of crisp, aging parchment. "Though if he was here, why didn't he find it himself?"

There was a loud crash and Tender jumped up from his seat. Tavera wheeled around instinctively to see what had made the noise. After a few breaths, Little emerged from the pantry area, a lopsided smile on his face. In his hands was a silver plate, shards of red pottery still encasing parts of it. "I found it."

Nausea rolled in the pit of Tavera's stomach as her eyes fell upon the plate, a lump forming in her throat. It had been found. They would be going. Tavera, called Point, was going to travel to an unknown place and hopefully rescue an aging priestess who desperately needed her help. Their help. Her eyes looked toward Tender, his own face taut with surprise.

"What…what do we do?" Tender rasped.

"Well…we have six days, correct?" Tavera asked. She tried to picture the layout of Ayilkin in her mind and the Freewild. "We don't know where Cy is."

"Little can track him," Tender offered. Tavera glanced over and Little nodded enthusiastically.

"Look, I don't doubt your brother's abilities as a tracker but a lot could happen in the next six days," Tavera mused. "It might rain. And the Freewild's a big place. I know. I've been through it. If the church sent her, they probably know where she came from. They probably know about this. Something about it, at least."

"Ayilkin proper is in the opposite direction of the Freewild," Tender said. "If we head into Ayilkin, we run the risk of running out of time."

"We've got six days," Tavera said, standing. "Did you not hear me? You been through the Freewild? It's big. It's constantly changing. A town thriving one summer might be abandoned the next. A border town would have the most recent information on what's there now, to guide our way. Better to back track and make one trip than wander about. That'll waste more time." Tavera watched as Tender nodded. "What temple was Sister Kella with before she came here?"

"Temple of the Moon in Morning," Tender said. "It's not far from the border of the Barony proper."

"If that's where she was before she came here, I'm sure someone will remember her. I doubt she was unknown," Tavera said. As soon as the words left her lips, she felt sorry too, remembering the look on the priestess' face, the desperation in her final call for help. "We'll get maps at the first town in, head to the temple and see what we can learn. Then a hard ride to wherever they say we should go?"

"I...I don't have any arguments," Tender said. He sounded resigned, the confidence he usually exuded absent from his voice. He turned to his brother. Little still held the silver plate in his hands. "Little?"

"I...guess...the plan makes more sense. Going blindly in rarely ends well," Little muttered. He stared down at the item in his hands.

"I'll go make arrangements. May Her black hand guide us all." The barkeep's voice sounded hoarse and he coughed, standing up and walking toward the open front door, disappearing into the morning sun. Tavera decided it didn't feel like morning and her stomach turned with nervousness. She looked down at the papers, hoping the busywork of trying to find clues in the drawings would distract her from her anxiety. Instead the images only worked her thoughts into a keen panic. When Little finally left, leaving her alone in the priestess' home, Tavera pushed the papers aside, praying to the Goddess she would not wind up like one of the gruesome pictures.

Chapter 8
Crossing Borders

Tavera was certain she didn't like riding horses. At least not by herself. Usually she rode in the backs of carts. When she did ride a horse, it was always with Derk in front. He was a good horseman, confident in the saddle and able to pick out a good horse and a good deal. But when she had been with Derk, time had rarely been of the essence. They had spent many a day sitting in the back of a cart full of goods, paying their way with money or forage in the Freewild. Sometimes Derk would sing a song if asked kindly enough.

The farmers and citizens of Whitend had offered their horses to the three of them for their quest. Little looked them over briefly before deciding on the three they now rode towards Reedsend. Tavera's was a black stallion named Blackie, of all things, and she worried the horse sensed her inexperience. Worse still, Tender kept glancing back at her. Every time he did, his horse would veer over and her horse would trot.

"You alright?" Tender asked, his brows furrowing. His horse veered again.

"Yes," she half hissed, pulling on the reins in an effort to slow the horse down.

"You look worried," he said.

"Well, I'm sitting on something that outweighs me ten times over, with a brain and desires all its own," Tavera said, looking down at the horse's large neck. Its black ears twitched as a fly attempted to land on one of them. "I'm imagining dying at the hooves of this thing."

"I doubt the horse has a murderous bone in its body," Tender said. "They eat plants, you know."

Tavera glared at him. "I know that," she said. "I'm just saying, a horse is a big animal and they can get away. I've heard stories of them bolting at the slightest scare. I heard a man got his head knocked off, riding a horse. Another person, broken in three places. Died later, the both of them."

"Let's not be giving the horses ideas, now," Tender laughed. "We don't need more gruesome tales." His face grew serious and Tavera frowned, realizing her brief stories were probably not what they needed right now. "How about some funny stories?" Tender prodded. "Something nice?"

"Not that much longer till Reedsend," Little called back. Tavera sighed with relief. Most of the trip they had gone in silence just the sounds of the Valley in spring and the horses accompanying them. They had rode the first stretch quickly, hoping to cover ground. When they had stopped to water the horses Tavera had busied herself with the journals, skimming them for clues. Tender seemed content to whistle and Little wasn't one for talk. The blond brother turned in his saddle, his horse snorting under him. "We should be able to see it once we get around this bend."

"Let's get there already then," Tender said, digging his heels into the side of his horse. Little made a chirping sound and his horse and Tender's took off, starting to trot down the road before breaking into a canter. Tavera tried to remember what Little had said. She gripped the horse's mane and tried to relax, making the same clicking sound with her tongue. The horse lurched forward and then began to speed after the others, going more quickly than Tavera would have liked. As the trio rounded the bend, the town came into view. The thought of dismounting made it easier for Tavera to bear the riding.

Little slowed his horse as they approached the entrance to the town, part of a wall and two brown-cloaks standing to either side of the road. Tavera ducked her head and tried to look inconspicuous. Her cap was in her saddle bag and she wished she could pull it over her hair and ears, at least for the moment.

"Who comes through, and from where?" the first guard asked. He was a freckled fellow with a shaved head and a red beard. "Freewilders, from the looks of it." He looked back at the other guard, a younger, dark-haired fellow. He looked so young, Tavera felt sure his mother packed the food he chewed as quickly as possible, trying to get his mid-day meal down.

"Freewilders, but only recently," Tender said. Little had arrived first but of course, Tender did most of the talking. "From Whitend. I'm Braxton Tender of that town, the bar-keep. We buy our incense for the temple here, in trade for beer. Perhaps you've partaken of it? Though you're new guards, right?"

"New to the post but not to guarding," the red-bearded one said. "Freewilders, eh?" He looked them over with blue eyes. Tavera watched his cloak flutter in the breeze, the hilt of his sword, the pinch of his helmet under his chin. He was still wearing his winter cloak. He'd probably been there since first watch and was tired, ready to take a break. "There's a gate tax," he said. "Half a blueie for each of you."

"How can you have a gate tax when you don't have a gate?" Tender scoffed. Both the guards stood up straighter, standing closer to the road.

"We're going to have a gate," the younger one said. "As soon as we can."

"As soon as you get enough people to pay the gate tax, eh?" Tavera muttered, holding on to her horse's reins. The red-bearded one looked her way but she just kept her head down, eyes on the dark, ebony mane of her horse.

"Well, gate or not," Tender said, "I'm here on church business and church business is exempt. Been this way in Ayilkin for the last ten years."

"Are you a member of the clergy?" the red bearded one asked. "You don't look the part."

"His tits are too small," the young one laughed.

"Just pay them," Little hissed. "Please."

"No," Tender said, looking to Little. "Our priestess was kidnapped in the dead of night by evil strangers and these two would have our blues? I won't pay and if they make us, may the Goddess have mercy on their souls, on these two who would hinder our way for a bit of blue! No gate will keep out Her judgment." Tender eyed the two guards from his seat, a dark eyebrow cocked at the pair of them. "Now, let us pass."

For a breath Tavera thought they would let them go, her good ear perking up at the possibility. But the young one stepped forward, swaggering as he stared up at Tender. "What proof do we have you're here on church business?"

Tender slid down from his saddle and approached the two men. He was obviously taller than the younger one and more confident than the red-bearded one. Tavera watched as he gave them both his most sincere smile and took the hands of the red-bearded one. "Then may the Goddess have mercy on my soul if I am lying about Her wishes to get out of a well-meaning tax." He smiled and slapped him on the shoulder before taking up the reins of his horse. "I used to be a brown-cloak myself so I understand. You're just doing your job. No one is blaming you. But we're here on church business and we know it's your job to respect that. Right?"

"And they're with you?" the red-bearded one said, looking to Little and Tavera.

"Naturally, yes," Tender said. "Now please, let us pass. Every breath we spend standing here trying to figure out if I'm lying or not is putting our priestess in more and more danger."

"If you're from the Freewild, your priestess don't fall under the mantle of the Church," the dark-haired one said, sounding pleased with himself.

"Just pay them!" Little hissed again. "Please, Tender, you're not even a real priest!"

The look Tender shot Little made Tavera turn her head to the side, trying to keep back the laugh. Tender's attempt to get them through the gate had almost worked. Little didn't look ashamed though Tender looked like he might cause his brother bodily harm. Tender quickly turned to the two guards, who now looked on the three of them suspiciously.

"I'm not ordained," Tender admitted, his hands gesturing as he spoke. "I'm the assistant to our priestess, and my mother, our mother," he said, pointing to Little, "served the church for many years before she went to be in Her bosom. It doesn't change the fact that our priestess, Sister Kella, a priestess of the Blessed Mother, assigned to the town just beyond your future walls just eight years ago, was taken from us by a strange man in...in very grave and cult-related business..." Tender paused. Tavera watched; he was trying to gauge the reactions of the guards. "She needs our help. We are going to the church to seek out that help. If we do not receive aid, I will be the one conducting services. Perhaps a service of the empty grave if you do not let us pass. By Her bosom," Tender pleaded, "let us go through. We've come from Whitend for help. Please. Please." Tender put his hands together. Tavera cocked an eyebrow at the barkeep, impressed. The two guards looked at each other for a moment.

"We'll let you pass," the red-bearded one said finally with a sigh. "Sorry to have kept you waiting." The red-bearded guard paused again before he shrugged. "Sister Kella said the prayer over my daughter on her Day of Blessing. I remember her. I'm sorry to hear she's come to such misfortune. Do you know who did it?"

"In a way," Tender answered, looking back to Little and Tavera. "We're hoping to get more information here. I'm hoping the priestesses here will have time for us."

"For such a concern, I'm sure they will," the red-bearded one said. "Please, pass through, though, no riding in the town itself. You must lead your horses through the streets."

"Of course," Tender said. Tavera slid down from her horse in relief, keeping the reins in her hands.

"And we'll need your names just the same," the dark-haired guard said. He pulled out a book and pen, setting it on a log meant to serve as a table. The book itself was new, just started since the last Baron's Day, Tavera guessed. All the people who had entered through on the main road to this town would be in that book.

"Right, I am Braxton Tender," Tender said. "And this here is my brother, Herix Tender." He watched as the dark-haired guard carefully wrote the names into the book. "And the woman is Point."

"Point?" the dark-haired man asked. Both of the guards looked to Tavera, obviously a bit confused.

"Point," Tavera said simply.

"Po...int..." the dark haired man wrote, giving her a strange glance as he finished. Tavera felt her face grow hot but she kept from showing any embarrassment or second-guessing. She should have thought of another name, she thought to herself. She could have said Point was her family name. Point wouldn't last as long as it should if Tavera gave it out at every gate. Little finally dismounted from his horse.

"And how long will you be here?" the red-bearded man asked.

"A day, at the most, we hope," Tender said. "We want to talk to the priestesses at the temple get a few provisions and then head out. Time is of the essence, unfortunately."

The dark-haired guard opened a drawer and pulled out three wooden passes. The red-bearded man pulled out a wax pen and wrote on them, handing one to Tender first. Tavera took hers and tucked it away. "You know how these work," the red-bearded guard said. "Try not to get them wet. Some pubs won't sell to you if you don't got a pass, so keep them on you."

"Sounds rude," Little said. Tavera thought the whole deal sounded suspicious but kept quiet. Not having a pass probably meant having a fine levied as well, she guessed. More money for the magistrate's coffers.

"We probably won't be out drinking," Tender said.

"Speak for yourself," Tavera chuckled, starting to lead her horse toward the city.

"You should check out the Verdy Arch," the dark-haired guard said, stepping back as the three of them led their horses past the guard posts. "Best fruit ale this side of the Holy Bowl."

"I'll be the judge of that," Tender scoffed.

"If you leave through the east gate for some reason, be sure to give them your passes on your way out!" the red-bearded one called.

"We know how passes work!" Little shouted back at them. "To Her hems with them," he growled. "They just became the last town of Ayilkin a few months ago. They sure took to it quickly! Acting like we don't know how to enter a town properly."

"Settle down, Little," Tender chided, leading his horse alongside him.

"Let him boil over," Tavera said. "I like it. It's nice to hear him talk for once." Little shot a glance at her that was supposed to make her shut up. Instead she laughed. "You hardly said a thing the whole way here. Some fapper with a beard calls you a Freewilder, your pants come off."

"It's because he was born in the Freewild," Tender whispered, obviously trying not to laugh.

"Don't tell her that, Tender!" Little hissed. "Shut up!"

"Oh, what's this?" Tavera asked, raising an eyebrow. "Is it true? Was you born in the Freewild?" The look on Little's face gave away the truth. "That explains a lot."

"It wasn't my fault," Little muttered. "I'd no say in the matter."

"I don't know about that," Tender mused, the three of them continuing down the street, passing the first homes of the town. "Mam went into the Freewild to oversee the vows of a few people. The only reason she went was because she was sure she had a few phases to go before you came. Lo and behold, as I stood by the town post on the day she was to be back, she never showed, not that day, nor the next. On the third day the town began to speak on sending someone out to find her when in the distance a cart showed up. In the cart was my mam and the ugliest baby I ever did see."

"Braxton, I hate you," Little huffed.

"Lies," Tender said, wagging a finger at his brother. "You love me. In any case, it seems he couldn't wait to get out. Must have been the Freewild air, calling to him."

"I do hate you, Braxton," Little growled again, though Tavera thought she could see a bit of a smile tugging at his mouth. Tavera was laughing by now too, enjoying the story.

"Don't worry, your secret's safe with me," Tavera chuckled. "I ain't one to judge."

"Aww, you're no fun," Tender said. "I was hoping you'd help me poke fun at Herix."

"If I was going to make fun of him for something, it'd be over something he had something to do with," Tavera said. "There's plenty there, just give me some time to warm up to him." She grinned at Little, who looked less thrilled to hear it before she looked up and down the main street. "So, where's the temple?"

"It's this way," Tender said. "To the right, just a ways down."

"They'll keep our horses for us," Little mumbled. "Their stable is well cared for."

"And where's the closest tavern?" Tavera asked, drawing an amused look from Tender.

"What for?" Tender asked. "You planning on going out for a drink?"

"No, I'm planning on having a meal," she said, looking over the shops on the main street as they guided their horses toward the temple.

"We can eat at the temple," Tender boasted. "Church business gets church food. The Goddess provides for those who do her work. If Sister Mereel is in the kitchen still, you're in for a treat."

"Not really here for treats, Tender," Tavera murmured. Her horse stopped suddenly in the middle of the street and Tavera had to pull on its reins to get it moving again. "Let's just ask the right questions and head out. We can make good time into the Freewild without riding too hard." She almost regretted admitting it. A hard ride to anywhere wasn't what Tavera wanted but why waste time in the town if they could get to the priestess with time to spare?

"I'd like to get to Kella as soon as possible as well," Tender said. "But these are ladies of the cloth. We can't just swoop in and demand answers. And we aren't expected. They might be busy."

"Too busy to answer questions that would save a fellow sister's life?" Tavera scoffed. "Tender, I hope you're joking. We're in more than a bit of a coop here. If the Sister's can't see to help us out, we need to figure out another plan."

"They'll help us!" Tender insisted. "They will. I'm just…a little…."

"He thinks you're going to embarrass him, I think," Little said.

"Is that so?" Tavera said, narrowing her eyes. Tender's face reddened slightly, even his ears. He looked more like Little when he was embarrassed. Tavera looked to the temple: a modest, whitewashed building with stairs leading to the round double doors. "You think I don't know how to talk to a priestess? Or sit in a pew? I've probably talked to more priestesses than you, Tender, just so yo--"

"Braxton!" Tavera looked up. A priestess stood at the top of the stairs, her long gray robes sweeping the floor. Her dark, curly hair was pinned back to show her face and ears, the wide neck of her vestments showing off her shoulders. Tavera noted the pretty rosary around her neck, the color in her cheeks, the way she looked into Tender's eyes. "What brings you here?" the priestess asked, smiling. The young woman looked to Little and then Tavera. "Who's this?"

"I'm Point," Tavera said. "And we're here on very serious business, Sister. It's urgent; can you tell us where your High Priestess is?"

"The High Priestess?" the woman said. She frowned slightly. "She's in Greenmere, visiting another temple. Why?" she asked, turning her face back toward Tender. "Is everything alright?"

"Greenmere?" Tender groaned. "That's a hard ride from here." Tender sighed. "Do you know when she'll be back, Cera?"

"She's not due till the end of the phase," Sister Cera said. Her thin brows knit with confusion. "Why, what's happening? Sister Pega is acting as the head while she's out. If you need church supplies, we can get them."

"It's not supplies we need," Little said. "Sister Kella has been abducted."

"What?" Sister Cera said. Her face went pale, disbelief in her eyes. "Abducted? Are you sure?"

"Very," Tavera said. "I was there when she was taken, Sister. Me and Tender tried to stop him but Sister Kella's abductor was…." She tried to think of the right word. Her memory went back to the sickle, the hard, red sheen on its curve, the strange lights and the dream. She couldn't think of a way to explain it without sounding unsure of herself. "He was very strong," Tavera said. It was true. She'd seen the way he hit Tender, how he seemed unaffected by Tender's blows. Tender was no slouch in a fight. Tavera still hadn't made sense of it. Perhaps the man called Cy had powers which made him stronger as well? "He took her on his horse and rode with her into the Freewild."

"We need the High Priestess," Tender said. "She knows more about Sister Kella than anyone else. She must know something about this, something that can help us."

"I can send a message to Greenmere for her, but I don't know how quickly the High Priestess will get here," Sister Cera said. "She is in Greenmere for a dissemination."

"Well, if she don't get back, we'll be doing a dissemination for Sister Kella and no one really needs that much liquor," Tavera quipped. "Let some other living person take care of the already dead and let's avoid adding to their numbers." Tavera shot a glance at Tender; he looked slightly embarrassed. Cera looked panicked. Good. "Please, Sister, do what you must. We only have six days."

"I'll send the message and then have Sister Pega come and see what she can do for you in the meantime," Cera said, nodding to herself. "Even if the High Priestess can't come back, I'm sure she can give us access to what you'll need to find her." She smiled at Tavera, a hopeful smile. "In the meantime, take your horses around to the stables. I'll meet you in the courtyard." Sister Cera took Tender's hand. Tavera watched the look that passed between them. Little looked away, suddenly more interested in the horses. "I'm sorry you're having to deal with this," Sister Cera said.

"Not as sorry as Sister Kella, I'm sure," Tender said. He let go of his horse's reins and placed his other hand on hers.

"I'll be back with Sister Pega as soon as I can," Sister Cera said. Her hands lingered on Tender's before she left, blushing slightly as she slipped away, heading to the front of the temple.

"Let's get these horses in the stable," Tender said. Tavera smirked at him, Tender frowning in response. "What?"

"Nothing," Tavera said. "I'm glad we have such a capable woman to help us."

Tender nodded, grabbing his horse's bridle. The three of them started walking toward the stables, Little leading the way. "Sister Cera's a good priestess. She's been here three years."

"Ah," Tavera said. "And how long have you been plowing her?" she asked.

The look on Tender's face made her laugh out loud.. "What?" Tender said. "I never! I mean. She's--"

"He's been circling the bed for a year," Little said, a hint of smugness in his voice. "Can't seem to mess the sheets."

"Little!" Tender hissed. Tavera laughed again. Little looked back, a smile of triumph on his face.

"No shame in taking it slow," Tavera reassured Tender. She patted him on the shoulder, Tender seeming relieved she wasn't making fun of him. "Just a whole barrel of frustration, I'm sure." She grinned at Tender, his face coloring at her words.

"It's just," Tender started. "I mean, you've been to Whitend! Cera's here, seeing to her duties. And I've got mine, with my bar and, well, looking after Kella. And Little." He pointed at Little accusingly. "I can't expect to pull her away from what she has to do and when I do visit, I'm not going to say, 'Oh, Cera, I'm here for the night, let's rub 'em together.'"

"'Rub 'em together'? Is that an east Valley saying?" Tavera laughed. She felt her cheeks starting to hurt from grinning. "Why not? She obviously don't just hold you in her heart, as they say."

"Now is the worst possible time to even be thinking about this," Tender huffed.

"Why?" Little scolded. "Do priestesses being abducted by crazed one-eyed cultists put you off your pleasure,

Brother?" Little scoffed, opening the stable door. "Really, the both of you."

"Eh, toss off, Little," Tavera said. "We can't be serious all the time. If you can't make a joke to lighten the load, the heavy crushes eventually, and we've got a heavy deal here. Better to crack a smile than get a crack in your spirit."

A priestess in gray-and-brown stable clothes came forward, taking the reins of Little's horse. "I guess you've a point," Little said, stepping to the side for Tender to lead his horse into the stable. "And truth be told, Tender could use a plowing."

"I hate you, Herix," Tender said through grit teeth.

Chapter 9
Find A Way

Tavera flipped her dagger over in her hand. She knew the activity was irritating Tender but she didn't care. She was doing it to keep herself occupied. They had been waiting in the courtyard of the temple complex for longer than they had anticipated. Tender sat on a bench, taking another slow mouthful of his soup. Any time someone walked by he would look up hopefully. This had happened several times, the stirrings proving to be other priestesses of the temple, going about their duties. Sister Cera hadn't passed by.

Little snored quietly on another bench. Around them were the well-tended trees and flowers of the inner courtyard, pink and white petals floating through the breeze. The remnants of their lunch sat on another bench, soup, white bean paste in bread, and sausages, which Tavera had declined. Tender had made a face at the beer they served but drank it. He took another slurp of his soup, his eyes focused on the ground and not the dagger Tavera flipped in her hand again. She flipped it again and noticed he winced slightly. He didn't trust her to catch it. Tavera threw it a bit higher and caught it. Tender turned away from her.

Out of the corner of her eye, Tavera saw the figure of Cera approaching, her steps quickly paced, scarves flowing behind her. Tavera tucked her dagger away and stood just a breath after Tender did. Tender smacked Little's hat off of his brother's face, rousing his brother quickly.

"What news?" Tender asked. Tavera heard a hint of nervousness in his voice, though she saw he was trying to seem collected. The look on Sister Cera's face told Tavera the news she had wasn't good.

"The messenger bird came back from Greenmere," Cera said. "The High Priestess is busy with the death of their High Priestess. They've asked she oversee the dissemination and choosing of the next High Priestess. In any case, she could not get here till tomorrow evening at the very earliest if she rode hard. Her health would not allow for that."

"Please, Cera, some good news?" Tender said. "We came all this way, we need something."

"She did say you may have access to the temple's library," Cera said. "I can help you maneuver the books and scrolls." Cera looked over their faces; they must have looked distressed. "In addition," she added quickly. "I suggest you go see Master Scritch. He specializes in maps, especially of the Freewild."

"How does he get maps of the Freewild?" Tavera asked.

"He pays people for their information," Cera said. "Simple as that. People will pay for accurate maps, especially of the Green."

"Fair enough," Tavera said. "I'll go see this map maker and try to get his most recent one."

"Why should you be the one to go?" Tender asked.

"I'm pretty good at getting good deals on things, truth be told," Tavera said. Little narrowed his eyes at her.

"Though…maybe I'll bring Little along with me," she added. "He knows the town."

"Not much use in a library anyway," Little said, picking his pack up and slinging it over his shoulder. "Can't read much."

"You sure?" Tender asked. "We could all go together."

"You worried I'm going to break him?" Tavera asked. "We'll go get the map and meet you at the library. Get a head start on that, we'll bring the other pieces."

Tender looked like he wanted to say no. Tavera picked up her pack and slung it over her shoulder, heading toward the exit. "It makes the most sense, Tender, we'll cover the most ground this way. Where's the map maker, Sister?" Tavera asked, walking backwards.

"On Keel Street," Cera called. "On the edge of the market square. It's got a compass on the placard." Cera frowned slightly. "Don't you want to keep your things here? We can store them downstairs so you don't have to carry them."

"No thanks, I like to have my things on me, Sister," Tavera said, casting a glance back to make sure she wouldn't trip. "Ready to go at a moment's notice."

"You better not leave, Point!" Tender said. His tone was jovial but something in his face told Tavera he thought she might.

"I ain't," Tavera called, spinning around. "Not unless Little's looking to leave you as well."

"I need a break from Tender," Little said. He actually smirked, his light eyes twinkling with mirth.

"Come back soon as you can," Tender called.

"I wouldn't dream of leaving you alone with Sister Cera for any long period of time, Braxton Tender," Tavera said, trying not to laugh while she said it. She grinned as they walked away from the two, making their way out of the temple and onto the street.

"So, the map? What's your plan?" Little asked.

"Easy," Tavera said. She looked around and tried to remember which way the edge of the market square was but Little was already heading off in one direction. She loped after him, considering her plan. "Get a recent map of the Freewild and if we can, one from the year Kella was originally abducted." Tavera walked alongside Little, looking over the layout of the streets, looking over the people over the town. "I'll look over Kella's journals and see where there's overlap, try to use that to sort out where Cy may have taken her."

"It would have been nice if Cy would have told us where to bring the cursed thing," Little huffed.

"The Temple of the Red Moon Rising is what we got and we'll figure it out," Tavera said. "We've got to. Even if it moved, someone will probably know where the members would have fapped off to. Probably." Tavera grimaced. How inconspicuous was a cult in the Freewild? A group of individuals with matching facial scars would be hard to hide. Then again, there were always things people kept their heads down about, especially in the Freewild Green. Tavera prayed someone had noticed, knew something which would help them find Kella.

The map store was surprisingly airy. Afternoon light poured through the windows, motes of dust spinning through the air. Plants grew in the windowsills, and on the back wall Tavera saw a fresco of Reedsend. Around it were other depictions of the town throughout the years, the boundaries larger with the passing of time. Wide cabinets lined the walls, no doubt holding already-drawn maps of various parts of the Valley. A tall, scrawny man with wiry hair sat behind the counter. He set down his pen and smiled at Tavera and Little as they approached.

"How can I help you?" the man asked, clearing his throat. "Are you in need of a map or are you here to sell information?"

"We need a map," Tavera said. Her eyes looked over the drawers and walls. Behind the counter was a curtain which led to what was probably a back room. A shadow passing under the curtain told Tavera someone was back there. "An old one, perhaps, and a new one."

"Heading to the Freewild Green?" the man asked with chuckle. He plucked a handkerchief from a back pocket, wiping his hands with the already-ink-stained square of fabric. "Well, I'll pay for any information you bring back. What region?"

"We're not sure," Little admitted. "Probably central."

"Do you have a map of temples in the Freewild, perhaps?" Tavera asked. "Other holy sites?"

"Is there one specifically you're looking for?" the man asked. He hopped off the chair and limped out from behind the counter. His limp was revealed to be the result of a wooden leg. The man grabbed a cane and walked over to one of the cabinets, an index finger running down the labels on the drawers.

"Temple of the Red Moon Rising," Tavera said. She couldn't help but grimace. Even saying the name sent her skin to crawl. The map maker raised an eyebrow and took his hands off the drawer.

"That's an old temple, to be sure. Doesn't exist anymore," he said. The way he said it told Tavera he believed it. "You going to dig about the ruins?"

"It does exist," Little said. "And they're going to kill someone there."

"What my friend means to say," Tavera interrupted, pushing past Little, "is we've been told to go there, and we mean to."

The map maker's eyebrows raised on his face, dark brown eyes wide. "Well, I'll have a map depicting the last known location of that cursed place," he said. "But if they've moved, I may not be able to help you. If you can avoid it, I would recommend it." He pressed his thin lips together in something close to a smile and shrugged. "I'll...I'll get the map for you." The old man hobbled toward the back room. "Gee!" he called before he disappeared behind the curtain.

Tavera listened as he spoke with whoever was behind the curtain. She sniffed and continued to look around, avoiding Little's eyes, straightening out her tunic and belt while she waited. She wondered what Tender and Cera were up to, what they had found in the library. Tavera still had to look over the journals. Perhaps she should have looked over them before coming here, she thought. But the map maker might have closed before she had finished. Maybe she'd go to a bar and go over the journals with some food. Get rid of Little and have some time to herself to sort out this part. That made sense.

Tavera leaned on one of the counters, looking at the intricately carved top. It was a carving of the Ten Crescents with the Holy Bowl laid at the left hand side, the Crescents winding their way down the length of the counter, inlaid with a beautiful material. The hometowns of the barons were depicted with their house colors, two-toned circles. Her eyes traced back to the Three Lake region, where the 'Wicks were. Where she had come from. Portsmouth was in Tyeskin Barony, where Gam lived. And Lights was down in Mielkin Barony. Derk...she traced her finger across the top of the carving, pulling her hand away.

The map maker emerged. Behind him came a woman who made Tavera look at her twice, the woman more interesting than the maps at the moment. She was dark skinned, darker than Tavera, darker even than the Forester Tavera had bedded what seemed like ages ago. The woman's wooly hair was pulled back atop her head in a bun. Her eyes were dark brown. The slight creases in her face and the way she held her mouth told Tavera she liked to laugh, though the woman was dressed in drab colors. Adding to her strangeness were her hands; despite the dark color of her skin, Tavera was still able to see black ink tattoos on her fingers and the backs of her hand.

"This is my assistant, Gee," the map maker said, seeing their faces.

"Gaela of Black Sands, more properly," the woman said. Her voice was higher than Tavera had expected. The woman named Gaela smiled at them, looking them over. She seemed as puzzled by Tavera as Tavera was by her.

"Black Sands? Where's that?" Little managed.

"South of here," Gaela answered. "South of your Forest of Clouds, south of the Red Plains. Down to where the grass dies away and there is only sand." Gaela meant for it sound mysterious, Tavera could tell. She enjoyed the look on Little's face. Tavera was curious as well but the map of the Freewild was what they were there for, not a geography lesson of the world outside the Valley. "We have many maps of the Freewild Green, but you will need more than that," the woman said.

"What else will we need?" Tavera asked.

"A map of the sky," Gaela answered. "To better help you navigate."

"If the cultists are still around, they may have built their temple in a location with the most astronomical significance," the map maker said.

"What?" Tavera said. Tavera had been following the conversation up until then. "What do the stars have to do with this? We know the eclipse is…of significance," she said, trying the word the map maker had used.

"The eclipse sets the date but for the things they do, for their location, they rely upon the stars to dictate where they should be," the map maker said. "What they are doing tonight is important but it is not their only dark ritual."

"How do you know all this?" Tavera asked, leaning away from the map maker.

The map maker looked down at the scrolls he and the woman named Gaela had brought from the back room. His eyes began to shine, tears filling them. "My cousin was once taken by them. Many years ago."

"Sister Kella?" Tavera asked. She knew it wasn't possible but it was close to the mark. The map maker looked up, his eyes wide. His wrinkled hands shook.

"No, but he was with her," he said. "He and three others, Kella included. They all went missing and we thought…we thought maybe a flood had taken them. Those happen in the Freewild in the summer, you know." The old man licked his lips, his face seeming older than just a few breaths ago. "But two summers after they had gone, my cousin came back. He was…he was a different man. He was…he was… disfigured." The map maker sat down on a stool behind the counter and Gaela put her hands on his shoulders in a comforting way, rubbing them with her tattooed hands. "He… he spoke of the temple and what they made him do and…." he said, his voice trailing off. "He said Kella was still there."

"Are you one of those who went to go rescue her?" Tavera asked. It was quiet in the room; the sound of a spring rain falling outside was the only thing she heard at the moment. The old man shook his head.

"No, not me," he said. "I couldn't go." He looked down at his leg, resting his hand on his knee. "And I didn't want to." The man sighed, looking up. There were tears in his eyes still but they didn't fall. "I wanted to spend time with my cousin. I had missed him, thought him dead. I wasn't going to leave him. And I'm glad I stayed. He died two phases after he came back." The map maker wiped his eyes with the back of his hand, sniffling hard.

"I'm sorry to hear about your cousin," Tavera said. She looked back at Little; he had removed his hat and stood solemnly, obvious concern on his face.

"I'm sorry for him and I'm worried about your friend who was taken," the map maker said.

"It was…Sister Kella who was taken," Tavera said. "We're going to rescue her."

"Sister Kella! By Her bosom, no!" The mapmaker stood there, mouth agape. "The sister, again? No, how could he?" Tavera saw the man trembled even worse. Gaela walked into the back room and returned with a bottle and several glasses, pouring the contents of the bottle into the glasses. Tavera smelled how strong the liquor was and thought about Kella and her habit. The map maker took his glass and sipped on it, the act of wrapping his fingers around the cup seeming to calm him down. "How is her assistant handling it? Tender's his name, right?" he asked.

"As well as he can be," Tavera shrugged. "He's back at the temple, trying to find out what he can do about it. This is his brother with me, he's coming with us to help."

The map maker shook his head, making a sad clucking sound with his tongue. He took another sip of his drink to steady himself, his face still sad. "I just can't believe it! Why did they take her again? How cruel can one man be?"

"They want something from her, they need something," Little said. "They said if we don't bring it, they'll kill her."

"Then you must give it to them!" the map maker said. "You must, for her sake. For the sake of my cousin who tried to save her, by coming back to the Valley and warning us."

"Your cousin," Tavera said. She tried to keep her voice steady, tried to keep the map maker from getting too emotional and unable to help them. "He came back and a party went out to rescue Sister Kella. He must have told them where the temple was."

"He did," the map maker said. He put down his cup and unrolled the map. "This red mark is where the temple was when he was first taken by them. This brighter red mark is where they were when he escaped from them."

"Two locations?" Tavera asked. "Why did they move?"

"They had to move where the light was, was all he told us," the map maker said, his voice tired. "It's been many years. They had several locations which they moved between. They could be at any one of them now. Well, Gaela can figure it out."

"I can consult my charts and get you a map of where they are likely to be," Gaela said. "Where are you staying? I can bring it to you by the high moon."

"We're staying at the temple," Tavera said. "We need it as soon as possible. We hope to leave at first light tomorrow morning. We've only got a few days to get there."

"Understood," Gaela said, nodding her head. She rolled up the maps and held them in her hands, smiling at the pair of them. "It shouldn't take long at all."

"What do we owe you for the maps?" Little asked. The map maker shook his head.

"No, no charge, not for you," the map maker said. "I couldn't. Not considering what you are getting into. Goddess bless you both, may Her Black Hand bring you back."

"May your words prove to be Her will," Tavera said, her stomach knotting. She took one of the glasses full of liquor and held it up for a toast. The map maker did the same and clinked his cup against hers, Tavera tossing her drink back. It was hot and dry and something about it reminded her of how parchment might taste if it was on fire. Little gulped his down; she saw him try not to shiver after he swallowed. Gaela hadn't poured herself a drink, which was just as well, if she was going to get to work on their map.

"We'll bring it by the temple," the man said. "We'll ask for--"

"Ask for Tender's crew," Tavera said. "Sister Cera is helping us with all this."

"Ah, Sister Cera is a good priestess, bless her," the map maker said. He nodded and sighed again, his mood more melancholy after their talk. "I'll have Gaela bring it by. If I don't see you before you depart, know you'll be in my prayers."

"Much appreciated," Tavera said, putting her cup down on the counter. "We should be going now, we've a lot to do before we set out."

"Understandable," the map maker said.

"I look forward to making your map," Gaela said with a nod of her head.

"Right, see you later," Tavera said. She and Little turned and left the shop, hearing the jingle of the door's bells after the door was closed. Tavera hooked her thumb under the shoulder strap of her pack. "That was either very good luck or very good manipulation," she said.

"How do you figure?" Little asked. Tavera walked after him, glancing over her shoulder, back at the shop.

"We just happen to get sent to a map maker who's familiar with the whole...ordeal." Tavera frowned slightly, thinking it over before she shrugged. "I'm not complaining. I think Cera knew the map maker would be of help."

"Well yeah, we needed a map." Little opened his pouch and pulled out a pipe, poking at the bowl with a dirty finger. "Though...I guess, yeah, him being the cousin and all. I suppose Cera knew. Though he is the only map maker in town, truth be told."

"I wonder about the woman who is working for him," Tavera murmured. She watched as Little filled his pipe, his light eyes looking about for someone who could give him a light. "You know. From...what was it, Black Sands? You ever heard of such a place?"

"Never," Little said. "But, well, where else do Valley folk know of? There's us, Freewilders? Foresters to the south, or right beside you if some strange bit of fortune has come to you," Little said with a smirk.

"Fortune?" Tavera said, returning his slight smile with one of her own. "And strange, at that? I feel like I should be on display."

"Elves don't wander about much. You're the first half-Forester I've heard of," Little said. He stopped at a food stall and had the cook light his pipe. The mix of tobacco he used was different from Derk's, but it reminded Tavera of her father all the same. His hands, rolling his cigarettes, the way they dangled from the corner of his mouth when he talked. The way he would stop mid-sentence to get a light during one of their conversations and pick up where they had left off. If Little noticed Tavera's nostalgia, he didn't say anything. "But Haranians to the east, an ocean to the west, the

Bones to the north. It don't matter. We don't need other people's business to keep us busy. We're fine keeping to ourselves."

Tavera nodded, thinking over what Little had said. True enough. Not having heard of Black Sands or seeing it didn't mean it wasn't there. Lights had never seen the Holy Bowl, being southern. As a child growing up in the 'Wicks, she could see the holy mountain on clear days. Black Sands... maybe she'd try to catch the woman named Gaela when she dropped off the map and ask her about it. "Speaking of keeping to ourselves," Tavera said, "I might stop by a bar on the way and sit for a bit and look over Kella's journals."

"Is my company that bad?" Little asked, exhaling a long stream of gray smoke.

"No," Tavera said, though she considered saying the opposite. "I could just use some time to sort through what we heard from the map maker and to look through Kella's journals."

"You can do that in the temple," Little said.

"I know I can," Tavera said, narrowing her eyes at him. "I just don't like their liquor selection," she managed with a straight face.

"What do I tell Tender if he asks after you?" Little said.

"Tell him to fap off if he asks after me," Tavera said. "You ain't my keeper. I'll be back before evening meal."

"Do you really want my brother going into every bar in Reedsend, looking for you?" Little asked. The way he said it told Tavera it was likely to happen.

"Just tell him I'm doing some research...there," Tavera said. She pointed at a bar farther down the street, its banner flapping in the wind.

"Good choice," Little said. "I know for a fact they have more types of beer than the temple."

Tavera rolled her eyes, trying not to laugh. "I'll be back. We can pool our information after evening meal. By then we should have the map and know what we'll need, where we're going."

"I'll probably try to get some provisions," Little mused, taking another drag from his pipe, trying to keep it lit in the light rain. "We've some money. I don't want to clear out the temple's pantry."

"Right, so I'll see you at dinner?" Tavera asked, raising her eyebrows. He nodded and Tavera chewed on the side of her mouth before she turned and headed into the bar. She looked back over her shoulder to make sure he wasn't watching her but he was already heading toward the market, pulling his hood up to protect against the rain. At least someone trusted her by herself.

Chapter 10
Bloody Pasts

The bar was like many other bars; Tavera felt her shoulders loosen as the heady aroma of sawdust, brewing beer, food and smoke filled her nose. The temple was a different sort of comfort. The smell of incense, the feel of wooden seats, the beauty of the carved statues affected Tavera differently than the sound of chairs scraping the floor, the warmth of bodies sitting around tables and the clink of glasses. To be in the temple was to be before the Goddess, to lay one's emotions bare for Her to see, for introspection. Bars were for making plans. For pulling in all the pieces while nursing a drink. Tavera nodded a greeting to the woman behind the bar and leaned against the bar top. "A mug of thinny and a roasted egg if you've got it," Tavera said.

"I've only got red eggs right now," the woman said, putting a glass on the counter. "Barleycakes,lady curls in oil and vinegar. I'll have whatever my son caught today roasting as soon as he gets back."

"I'll take the greens," Tavera said, pulling out her purse. "How much?" she asked, watching as the barkeep filled her glass.

"Two blueies," the woman said. "Want me to tell you when we've got meat on the fire?"

"No, thanks," Tavera said, putting the coins on the counter. She thought for a moment. "Let me get a pitcher of thinny, actually."

"Five blueies then," the woman said, watching as Tavera put them on the counter. "Rough day, girl?"

"Quite a few rough days, all in a row," Tavera admitted, managing something of a grin. The bar woman laughed and poured the cup of beer into a pitcher, topping it off and handing it to Tavera.

"Greens on the house," the barkeep said, smiling. "But don't go telling everyone. If I gave things to everyone having a shit day, I'd be out of beer before moonrise."

"Your secret's safe with me," Tavera chuckled, taking the pitcher and the now empty glass.

"I'll have your greens out soon as I can get them in a bowl," the barkeep said.

"No rush, just can't spoil my evening meal," Tavera sighed, laughing. "I'll be over there." She pointed with the pitcher when she said it, indicating a booth off to the side. Tavera sat at the table, setting the pitcher down and pouring herself a glass before she opened her pack.

There were six journals in all. Tavera made sure the table top was clean before she set out the journals, not wanting to stain their covers with beer or food. A cursory glance around the bar told her no one was watching her. Reading several books in a bar might draw attention, she realized but at the moment it seemed the bar was underpopulated. She'd be gone before it started to fill up for evening meal.

The oldest journal was bound in leather, its pages the most discolored with time. Tavera opened it, noting the even handwriting, the careful penmanship. This was probably from before Sister Kella was abducted, Tavera reasoned. Tavera wanted to read it, in the hopes of seeing the type of person Sister Kella was before the cultists had changed her.

Tavera sighed and turned a few pages in the journal, skimming the words, trying to glean a bit from the personal diary. A splotch of ink stopped Tavera as she turned the pages, cocking her head to the side. She took a sip of her drink and turned another page, seeing another splotch of ink. Without reading, Tavera turned the next few pages. It looked like someone had deliberately ruined some of the entries in the journal, dark ink spilling over entries, making their contents unreadable. She frowned, running a finger over the stained pages, wondering what had been erased and why.

Four journals were bound books, leather covers protecting the pages, signatures sewn into the spine with a decorative pattern. Two of them were simple uncut journals, single pieces of paper, folded many times with book ends slipped onto the outermost pages. If they had cases, they hadn't been in Kella's trunk. These were less expensive journals, probably purchased from a stall somewhere in Ayilkin Barony.

Tavera picked them up and turned them over, noting the circular seal on their backs. The workshop would have marked the journals they made. Tavera didn't recognize the seal. Not too surprising. Journals and books weren't things she paid attention to generally, but she noted this one. Two herons facing each other, necks bent so their beaks touched, forming a heart shape. Tavera turned to the first page.

Second phase of the second month of spring, year 132 of the Valley's reckoning. I forgot my journal back at my home temple and have purchased two fold journals in the market. I have to keep a record of our trip across the Valley! I have

never been to the western Valley before and am excited to
embark with Wing and the others. Wing tells me the mar-
ket of Tyestown is dyed every color one can imagine. I'm
hoping the rains dissipate in the next few days; the Mother's
Splendor is said to be breathtaking under a full moon and it
would be a shame to miss it because of a few clouds. The
benediction is tomorrow however, and so we are all excited
for that, overcast or not.

Tavera's brows furrowed. The Mother's Splendor was in
Whitfield. Directly outside the walls was a proliferation of
the most beloved flower in the Valley, the moonflower. It
grew best on disturbed soil and overran graveyards
throughout the region, crawling across the earth with its
heart-shaped leaves. The round buds bloomed in spring, always at night for a few days around the full moon. Small,
white flowers, the size of a fullie seemed to glow under the
moonlight and while many spots in the Valley were known
for having their own spectacle of flowers, Whitfield was the
most popular.

The head of the church lived in Whitfield and would
give a benediction on the full moon, with many gathering
to hear her speak. Tavera wondered who Wing was. Was
Wing the cousin of the map maker? Tavera turned the page
to read the next entry, nodding and mouthing a 'thank you'
as the barkeep left her bowl of greens at the table.

There were several illustrations, rather artfully done. Tavera
raised her eyebrows at the depictions of the Her Luminance
giving the benediction, a coil of moonflower wrapped around
someone's hand. A woman's face, the corners of her lips curled
upward slightly. She didn't wear her hair like a priestess. Under
the portrait was written 'Wing of Little Bend.'

The next page held two more portraits, these of two
men. One had a long, saturnine face, the brush-strokes sug-

gesting dark hair and a calm demeanor. The other man had a crooked nose but a smiling mouth, his head cocked to the side. Their names were Regick and Deril, apparently. Tavera thought the one with the crooked nose looked more like the map maker. They had the same curly hair and mouth, though their jawlines were different. Then again, she thought, looking at the darker man, perhaps he was the one. They could be cousins by vow and not by blood. Either way, they had all been taken by the cultists, all of them missed. And now one of them had been taken, taken away again.

Tavera turned the page. A journal entry about the benediction, the High Priestess blessing them on their journey, Wing and Reg getting into an argument over how much food to pack. Pictures of landscapes ran across the top of the pages, framing Sister Kella's careful and measured script. Words of rain and anxiety over sleeping out of doors for the first time alongside an image of Deril playing a stringed instrument. An entry read:

Too much rain. Cart stuck in the mud. Not sure how we'll get it out.

The writing was smudged, probably from water damage. Dirt was smeared at the edges of the pages. The map maker had mentioned flooding that year. Tavera touched the pages, for some reason expecting them to be wet. She imagined the four of them, huddled together, their cart stuck in the mud, their animals probably miserable. Tavera remembered cold, wet days with Derk, sniffling under cloaks, trying to get fires started. At least they'd had each other for company. Tavera wondered what jokes they'd told under whatever shelter they'd made to lighten the mood. If Deril had sung a song or Kella a hymn. When had the cultists attacked? At night when they were asleep? Or had they ambushed them while they shivered around a fire, heavy rain drowning out their ominous approach?

Tavera took a bite of the greens as she turned the next page, her chewing slowing as her eyes fell upon the words.

They don't know I have this but I have to record this. They have captured us all. Not sure where others are. Wing is with me, Thank the Goddess.

The water is drugged. Trying not to drink it. Goddess, give me strength.

Saw Deril today, Holy Mother, what have they done to him? Wing screamed. Give me strength.

They took Wing from me. I hear her crying in the other room. I thought she was the strong one. The water is drugged.

Deril came to see me. Mercy upon him, Goddess, help him. Why has this happened?

Wing sang a song with me today. They gave her back to me. I'm so happy.

Wing is dead. She killed herself. What could I have done to stop her? What could I have done? What could I have done? What? What? What?

Tavera turned the page. Someone had poured ink on the next page. The writing she could make out was scrawled. The splash of the black liquid looked like blood. The ink that had soaked through had made the pages stick together a long time ago and it looked like someone had pulled them apart before Tavera.

Tavera ran her fingers over the page, to see if she could feel the words on the page but they had been written so long ago in graphite and stains. What she saw was more of the same: short entries, the handwriting worse. Tavera was convinced Sister Kella herself had blotted out these books, trying to forget what had happened. Her firsthand account, stricken from the record by her own hand in the hopes it would clear her memory. But it hadn't. Hence, the stack of journals written after the fact, the recollections, the bad handwriting, the drinking.

The second fold journal was more of the same. Blotted out pages though Tavera made out the frantic handwriting, the sketches, marred with black. Tavera wondered why Sister Kella never rid herself of the journals, never burned them. She had taken them to wherever her rescuers had borne her to and then carried them with her, kept them in her trunk in her little home in Whitend. Did she look them over, reliving them? Or did she keep them locked away tight, feeling secure with their placement in the trunk?

The thing Tavera had owned the longest was the pin with the big blue head Derk had got for her all those years ago, before he had taken her on, and the rest of her lock picking set. Derk had always had his dagger. Fun things, useful things, things that got one out of trouble, not reminded her of bad times. Though Tavera still had the piece of gold ribbon from her initiation. It reminded her of Derk being cut away from her. It was buried in the bottom of her pack.

Tavera flipped through the other journals. A journal that started off as landscapes and portraits only was next. There was an image of a graveyard; Tavera recognized the temple they were staying at. She ate her food while she flipped through the images, looking over the drawings. As the images went on, Sister Kella's hand grew steadier. Tavera noticed the familiar folds of the priestess' garments, their braided hair. Most of them were labeled. Sister Berka, Sister Derseel, Sister Pega. Next to a drawing of one woman, labeled Sister Mika, Sister Kella had written 'I hate her.'

Tavera frowned. The next page showed a journal entry.

They want me to write about my time there. Sister Gilra says it will help me. That what happened must be exposed. But I don't want to. I don't want to share it. But I must talk to someone and no one here understands. They all treat me like an outcast. Like I helped Cyric. But I did. I had to. And I miss them. Or rather, I lack them. Being in the Valley is so strange. No one tells me what to do and my mind wanders and I think of him. And of Wing. Everything has been taken from me. What do I hold on to?

Tavera finished her meal and turned through the pages. Pictures of the priestesses. A portrait of Cyric, criticisms and curses written in large, dark letters. *Cruel. Controlling. May your soul go toothless to Her Hems. Disgusting. Cursed.* The temple was depicted. Various buildings in Whitened, drawn so well Tavera recognized them despite her short stay. The courtyard where she and Tender and Little had waited for Cera, its trees smaller. The Goddess cradling someone in her arms.

A desolate scene of burning buildings. A woman lying on the ground, a dark smudge of ink around her neck, a shard of something in her hand.

She wanted to cry. Tavera took a deep breath, turning another page, feeling the brittle pages holding so much emotion, so many terrible memories. Tavera remembered Kella's face, the creases in her skin, the look in her eyes. Growing up on the Blocks and in the Wicks, Tavera had led a rough life but nothing as bad as this. Never seen her friends killed. Never been tortured, kept prisoner. And once she was with Derk, never forgotten, passed over.

All the time Sister Kella spent alone in her room, did she think of Cyric? The priestess had known he would come that night. What was she hoping to get, meeting him in secret? Tavera opened the pages of the later journals and looked over the drawings of Cyric. Some of these showed him in a gentler light, the scar across his face less menacing. What had happened that allowed Kella to hold two images of this man in her mind?

Tavera flipped to the front of the next journal, seeing the image of the sickle sketched in black and red inks on the paper. More time seemed to pass between each entry. Some entries were simple retellings of the day. Drawings of more priestesses, more landscapes. Memories redrawn, each passing illustration fuzzier and fuzzier, though still as full of sadness and pain. Wing showed up again and again, usually with a drawing of Cy on the same page or on the opposite. Stains in the lettering suggested tears shed. Several suggested wet mugs had been placed on the pages to hold them down.

What did the journals tell Tavera about Cy and the cultists? Whatever they had done to Sister Kella, it had affected her greatly. The pain she endured and the guilt she must have felt after her friend had died must have been too much to bear, yet Sister Kella had held on. Why? All she had was her congregation and, it seemed and from Tender's accounts, she didn't seem to take her duties too seriously.

After years of abuse at the hands of Cy and the other cultists, what was her abduction? Revenge? The red moon was a time to pay debts and return wrongs, though most churches greatly encouraged non-violent reckoning. Did Cy think he was bringing her home? He wanted the plate, obviously, but why take Kella? Why not have her find it?

The bar door opened and Tavera smirked as Tender entered, gazing around the bar until his eyes found Tavera, nodding in her direction. He squeezed in across from her, giving the journals a cursory glance. "Little said I'd find you here."

"Did he?" Tavera asked. "I thought you'd just check every bar in town until you found me." She picked up her drink, flipping through the pages again to look over the illustrations. "Shouldn't you be with Cera?" she asked, taking a sip. It was hoppy and floral, a good drink for spring.

"Why, are you jealous?" he asked. Tender grinned. Tavera managed not to roll her eyes at his stupid jest.

"No, I just thought we had a job to do," she said. "Besides, what do I have to be jealous of? That you're able to like two girls at once? It's hardly a difficult task."

"Look, besides that," Tender said, changing the subject. "What're you doing in this bar? You should come back to the temple. Evening meal is about to start."

"I know what time of day it is," Tavera sighed. "I'm just looking things over in a more...comfortable location."

"Comfortable?" Tender asked. "What's more comfortable than the temple?"

"A place I'm more used to," Tavera said.

"You've never been to this bar before," Tender rebutted, smiling before taking a sip of his beer. He made a face and held it in his cheeks before swallowing.

"I've been to so many bars throughout the Valley and you know what I've learned?" Tavera said. "They're basically the same. A door you walk into, a keep behind the bar, liquor, beer, wine. Maybe a stage. They all smell like beer and food and are warm inside." Tavera wondered if Sister Kella had made it to the cultist's temple and if she found any of it comforting. The smell of Cy as he held her close to him, as they rode off. They would be in a different location. Would the difference be unsettling or a welcome change? Would it be disorienting?

"Temples are the same for me," Tender offered. "And the priestesses at this temple are very kind indeed. They lead their congregation well."

"I don't doubt it, Tender, but I'm not of temples. I go to them. But that's not all my life. My place is in the pews, not behind the altar."

"What do you think of my temple, then?" he asked, smiling. "Bar and temple? Is it like a dream come true for you?"

"Not my dreams," Tavera laughed, looking at the table. "No."

"What do you dream of?" Tender asked.

"A man," Tavera admitted. This was true.

"Someone I know?" Tender asked, his eyebrows raising on his face.

"A man I plowed," Tavera said, watching as Tender smile faded. "Very handsome. Tall. Dark hair, dark eyes. Scars I could run my hands over. Do you know him?"

"Probably not," Tender murmured sheepishly, blushing slightly. "Sounds nice, though."

Tavera just shrugged. They sat there for a moment in silence. Tavera flipped through the pages of the journals. She thought of the terrible dream Cy had given her. She was convinced Cy had pushed it into her mind, with his terrible sickle. She remembered the sparks, how they had cascaded off the edge of the terrible blade. There was no mention of anything like that in the journal, not that Tavera saw initially.

It wasn't Wielding, what the Valley called magic, at least Tavera didn't think so. Wielders didn't use tools in the stories Tavera had heard. He wasn't a spirit summoner. Priestesses prayed and lit incense and counseled but acting as vessels for the Goddess was seldom done and couldn't be commanded. It was deliberate, what he had done. He knew what he was doing when he pointed the sickle at Tavera and knocked her into that terrible…whatever that was. What could he be mixing in Sister Kella's mind? What memories and fears could he conjure and inflict upon her? And how could they stop him from doing it again?

Tavera looked up from the books at Tender. "So." She poured herself another cup of beer. "I'm going to finish up here and I'll be back for evening meal."

"Alright," Tender sighed. "We'll talk when we get together." He drummed his fingers on the table top before he stood. Tavera just chuckled to herself as she watched him go.

Tavera looked over the stack of journals and put her head in her hands. All she knew after looking over them more closely was that Kella was indeed in danger, and that if they didn't help her, there was no telling what Cy would do to her. She hoped the priestesses would have information which would save Sister Kella from further torment at the hands of the bloody cult.

Chapter 11
New Allies

Tavera slung her pack over her shoulder and hopped down the steps leading up to the bar, looking up and down the street. Stores were winding down, the owners wanting to get home for evening meal before vespers. Food stalls were always the last to close, the farmers selling the ingredients needed up until the last minute, usually eating some of the wares for their own meal. Colorful heartberries in baskets scented the air as Tavera walked by, and the aroma of grains being toasted made her stomach growl. The vegetables she had eaten had been good but not enough.

Tavera stretched her fingers, cracking her thumb knuckle as she approached the closest cart, looking at the bucket she intended to sample from and the owner. A light drizzle was falling from the sky so the robust man with the fuzzy red eyebrows was trying to stay out of the rain. A man and woman also approached the cart from the opposite direction, the man wrestling with the child he held in his arms. "Be good," the man said. "If you want your ma to make you a treat, stop squirming." The little boy seemed to take this as a challenge and starting wiggling more, laugh-ing as his father tried to hold him and keep a straight face.

"If I only made sweets when he was a good boy, we'd never get sweets," the woman laughed. She already had her purse out, probably wanting to make the transaction as quick as possible, the vendor already drawing near. He didn't notice Tavera open her belt pouch and come over, picking up a few berries and dropping them into her purse. They'd get bruised that way but it was a small price to pay. Her heart thumped as the vendor looked her way, eyebrows furrowing. She waved at him with the hand she had just used to pilfer the fruit, smiling at him, being sure her cloak covered the opened pouch.

"They smell wonderful," she said. He nodded a thank you and then turned back to the couple, counting out the berries they asked for, the woman offering a small cloth bag to place them in. Tavera turned and started walking away, feeling eyes on her. Tavera continued down the street, knowing better than to look back just yet. She kept her pace and closed her purse, looking over the other stores and stalls lining the street.

A stall selling scented water and oils was still open. Stalls that sold goods tended to be more open to customers spending time looking at their wares, while food vendors generally chased people away if they lingered. Tavera of-fered half a smile to the woman sitting behind the makeshift counter. "I can make you a custom scent," the woman said, her wide-brimmed hat making her face look small.

"I don't doubt it," Tavera said, looking over the small clay jars labeled with words and pictures. She picked up a vial and looked at the picture. Beer burr. A picture of the pale green, scaled plant was painted on the side of the vial. Tavera removed the cap and sniffed. It was less bitter than it tasted, more floral, bright. Tavera put it back and decided to look in the direction where she had come from now, mouth pursing as she spied who was most likely watching her. The woman from the map shop was at the fruit stall, buying some heartberries. When she was done paying the man she turned and waved to Tavera, smiling brightly as she jogged over.

"I'm glad I caught you here," Gaela said. Tavera saw she had something slung over her shoulder, a long tube with a leather strap. She held a small basket of heartberry in her hands. "I have the maps you asked for."

"That was quick," Tavera said, turning away from the stall and avoiding the seller's irate expression.

"We've got a powder that helps the ink dry faster," Gaela admitted, apparently not willing to take any of the credit for herself. "And the maps weren't hard to pin down. The star map was the hardeest of the three."

"I see," Tavera said, starting to walk down the street, Gaela walking alongside her. She was shorter than Tavera and her hair was wrapped in a piece of fabric. Within her hood Tavera saw earrings on her ears, made out of something Tavera didn't recognize. Gaela glanced at Tavera and Tavera realized she was staring, and felt her face grow hot. Gaela held the basket of heartberries out toward her.

"Would you like one?" Gaela asked. Tavera smiled and took one, seeing Gaela smirk slightly. "It's hard to eat just a few, isn't it?"

Tavera took a bite and looked at Gaela out of the corner of her eye. "Good thing you bought more than a grip," Tavera said, finishing the berry and tossing the green leaves to the ground.

"I saw you take from that man's stall," Gaela said quietly. Tavera kept walking at the same pace, trying to gauge why Gaela was telling her this.

"Did you?" Tavera asked. "Take what?"

"You took five berries from the lower basket."

If Derk was accused, he would laugh. That's how Derk was. Tavera just let the silence drag on, walking down the street toward the temple. If Gaela had wanted to, she could have said something during the act but hadn't. She wanted Tavera to know she had seen it but didn't seem too troubled about it. She hadn't accused her right away. "Did I?" Tavera said finally. She smiled at Gaela, a side-ways smile. "Stranger things have happened. What's your point?"

"Why did you take them?" Gaela asked. Her words rang not with accusation but curiosity. Tavera puffed out her cheeks and blew out a long breath, wishing she had pockets to stuff her hands into. Maybe she should just run. She couldn't, though. Gaela knew she was staying at the temple and they needed the maps. Better to sort this out and then see what happened.

"Because I wanted to," Tavera said.

"Is Point your real name?" Gaela asked.

"Yes," Tavera said. "Any other inquiries?" she asked, tak-ing another berry from the basket.

"Do you do what you want?" Gaela asked. She asked quietly, almost in a whisper. Tavera looked at her hands holding the berries before she looked at the ground.

"Generally, yes," Tavera said. "Especially as of late." She let that last bit hang in the air for a moment, leaving it open for interpretation. Gaela turned to her, a slight smile perk-ing at the sides of her mouth.

"I want to go with you to save the priestess," Gaela said.

Tavera almost stopped in her tracks. "What?" she said. "No, you don't," Tavera laughed. "You don't know what you're getting into."

"Do you?" Gaela asked. Tavera avoided her gaze and then scrunched her face up, turning down a side street to lengthen their trip to the temple, hoping to talk this out.

"More than you do," Tavera said. "Tender and I have dealt with this man who's taken her and, well..." Tavera looked around and then raised her eyebrows at Gaela, leaning in closer to Gaela to keep her words unheard by others. "The man who has taken Sister Kella is able to use...." Tavera didn't know what to say. She wasn't even sure how he had done it. "Something like Wielding."

"Something like it?" Gaela asked. They had stopped in a back alley and Tavera perked up her good ear and make sure no one else was within earshot. "You mean like how you made sure no one in the market saw you take those berries?"

"Not like that at all," Tavera said, not appreciating the joke. She looked to Gaela, who wasn't laughing. "This is real power, not sleight of hand or diverting attention."

"You mean like this?" Gaela asked. She held her hand up toward a wooden crate, pointing two fingers at it. Tavera watched as Gaela squinted, her hand shaking while still pointing at the box. Something made Tavera's ears twitch though she couldn't hear anything, except for the sounds from the main street growing quieter. Tavera held her breath and then jumped. The wooden box fell apart, a pile of splinters on the back alley ground.

Tavera struggled with words, her mouth hanging open in shock as Gaela sucked in a deep breath, fog slipping past her lips when she exhaled. Tavera realized she was leaning against another crate, gripping the corner of it with her hands. A splinter pierced her skin and she brought it to her mouth, still amazed over what she had just seen.

"What? What did I just see?" she asked, realizing how silly it sounded once she said it. Gaela thought for a moment, picking up the basket of berries she had set down.

"Something like Wielding. We don't call it Wielding where I'm from, and I don't think it's the same...concept?" Gaela mused for a moment, looking at the pile of sticks. "It's like making a fire from flint and tinder, instead of moving a burning log from one hearth to another. Both make fire but they're different. Do you see?"

Tavera frowned slightly, thinking over the example given. They were different, she understood that. But how it applied to what she had just witnessed...Tavera looked at the splinter in her finger. "Which one was you doing, the flint or the log?"

"The log," Gaela said, in a voice meant to be reassuring. Tavera raised her eyebrows at her.

"Can you take this splinter out?" Tavera asked. "Perhaps with less...exploding?"

"Of course!" Gaela put the basket down and held out her hands. Tavera offered Gaela her own, not sure what she was getting herself into. She felt Gaela's soft hands on hers; Tavera closed her eyes, wondering if she hadn't made a mistake, envisioning a bloody hand. She winced as she felt a pinch and then a yank. Tavera opened her eyes and frowned. Gaela held the splinter in a small pair of tweezers, smiling at her.

"What the Tits, I could have done that!" Tavera exclaimed, pulling back her hand.

"Then why'd you ask me?" Gaela asked. She cleaned the tweezers on her cloak and returned them to the pouch she wore at her waist.

"I thought you'd use...what you did, maybe to get it out." Tavera rolled her eyes at herself, starting to walk down the

street. "Can't you heal? Can you close a wound or fix a broken bone?"

"My understanding of anatomy is good enough. I could
probably help with something like that, if given time." Gaela
nodded as they walked, not caring that Tavera had taken
another berry from the basket. "But I can't just do it all the
time, use the power. Just like you can't take from everybody
to get everything you need."

"True enough," Tavera mused, feeling the rain start to
fall more heavily just as the temple was in sight. "Though it
does taste better when I do take it myself." She smiled at
Gaela and the smile Gaela returned told her the woman
knew what she was talking about. "Well, I want you to go
with us. Cy's not expecting it and we need all the kinds of
help we can get."

"Good!" Gaela said. "I know the stakes are dire but I do
want to help. After hearing the map maker's story, I'd feel
terrible knowing I was able to help but didn't."

"I'm hoping Tender will see it the same way," Tavera
huffed, managing a nervous grin in Gaela's direction. The
steps to the temple stood before them but Tavera sighed,
looping her arm in Gaela's and leading her toward the side
entrance, where they were meant to go.

"Who's this?" Tender asked. Little looked up from his
plate, eyes growing wider as he saw Gaela again. Tavera let
her pack fall to the ground with a thump before she sat at
the table, leaving a space for Gaela to sit by her.

"Gaela of Black Sands," Tavera said, trying to make it
sound like she knew all about Gaela and Black Sands. She
cleared her throat and contemplated the food. More spring
salad, barley bread, eggs in broth, and beans. "She's the map
maker who's helping us."

"The woman you were speaking on, Little?" Tender asked. Little nodded.

"And what exactly did Little say?" Tavera asked. She put a plate in the spot beside her, Gaela finally sitting down next to her before she served herself some soup.

"That she was a sky mapper and worked for the map maker," Tender said. "As a helper."

"If she made the map, ain't she a map maker?" Tavera said.

"I did more than help him," Gaela chimed in finally, her hands in her lap. "I did most of the maps and the indexing during the last few months. Most of the maps we've sold the last three seasons have been done by my hand."

"Why's he saying you're his helper then, if you're doing the work?" Little spoke up.

"Well, I'm a stranger here," Gaela admitted. "People feel more confident in a map made by another Valleyman than a foreigner."

Tender smiled at Tavera. "Well that was nice of you, inviting her for evening meal, as a way of saying thanks."

"Actually, she wants to come with us," Tavera said. She faked a smile at Tender, his own smile melting from his face at her words.

"What?" Tender said. "No. Why?"

"She says she can help us and I think she can," Tavera said. After seeing what Gaela had done in alley, her maps could be crap for all Tavera cared. Having someone with Gaela's abilities wasn't a bad thing, especially given the unknowns in the situation. "We're going up against quite a few people. Another head isn't something we should be turning away. Not to be rude, but I don't exactly see anyone in gray offering us much in bodily support."

"Why would she want to help us?" Tender said, pointing to Gaela but speaking to Tavera. "She don't know the sister. And it's going to be dangerous, we can guarantee that."

"Because I want to help," Gaela said. "I don't have to know the sister to know she's in a terrible situation. No one should be trapped by people they're afraid of." Gaela looked at her empty plate, her eyes growing sad. "After you left, the map maker began to cry in the backroom, weep-ing for Kella and his cousin and the others they had lost. I told him I would ask to join you, to help when he couldn't and he said if you would have me, I might go. Your success is important to more people than just you three and the sister."

Tender sighed, pouring himself another drink. Tavera ate and watched, seeing Tender slowly begin to accept Gaela into their group, knowing they could use another person. "Can you swing a sword?" he asked, taking a sip of his beer.

"Well, if we're going to be honest, you can't swing a sword," Little muttered, poking at his own food. Tender shot Little a look, Little shrugging in answer. "Swinging a club ain't the same as a sword, Braxton, it just isn't. Hitting a man in the head isn't running him through."

"You can't swing a sword?" Tavera asked, the confidence she was starting to grow dropping considerably. "Weren't you a browncloak?"

"We used clubs even then," Tender said, trying to make it sound like a matter of pride. "I'm more than capable with a club. Or a table leg. Large branches."

"Maybe we ought to leave you here with the priestesses and take Gee with us," Tavera laughed.

"It's Gaela, please," Gaela said. She reached over and took the bowl of salad and served herself.

"Sorry, Gaela it is," Tavera said. "Look, Gaela can help us. Show 'em." Tavera started in on her soup, still hot and steaming, slices of egg floating in the earthy broth.

"Show what?" Little asked, alarm in his voice. "What is she going to show?"

"Calm down, Little," Tavera said.

"Maybe now's not a good time," Gaela said. "A priestess might walk in."

"What is she going to show us?" Tender asked, putting butter on his bread.

"You have to do something," Tavera said, talking with food in her mouth. "Come on."

"Okay," Gaela said. Dark eyes scanned over the table, settling on Tavera's soup. Tavera stopped eating, and edged away from Gaela. She looked to Tender, cocking an eyebrow at the woman.

Gaela's fingers bent in a strange gesture, palm facing the bowl while she concentrated. Tavera looked around, the sound in the room seeming to wane again while the surface of the soup rippled. Nothing else on the table moved. Little mumbled something under his breath. Something emerged from the surface of the bowl of soup, a gray mist settling into the palm of Gaela's hand. Tavera leaned forward and tapped the surface of her bowl with a spoon.

"It's frozen," Tavera said.

"What?" Tender said, reaching over and picking up the bowl of soup. Tavera rubbed the tips of her fingers together and looked at the swirling cloud spinning over Gaela's palm. She reached out and put her hand over Gaela's, feeling the heat rising off of it, the heat from her soup drifting upward into the air, snaking around Tavera's hand.

"By all that's green and good," Little whispered. Tavera looked at him and moved her hand, the heat slipping up and dissipating into the air. Tender still held the bowl of soup upside down.

"By Her bosom," Tender gaped. "A Wield-"

"No," Gaela said. "I'm not one of your Wielders. I make magic taught to me by my mother, the magic of those from Black Sands, from the Thousand Boats of the Blessed. I'm asking to come with you. Please, let me help. No one should be forced to stay where they don't wish to be."

Tender put the bowl back on the table. He was trying to find some way to say no, Tavera could see it in his face, the way he didn't look at Gaela. He looked up finally, eyes narrowed slightly. "Do you believe in the Goddess?" he asked.

"That shouldn't matter," Little spoke up, sitting up straight on the bench. "If Gaela is willing to help, we should have her."

"Let's not forget," Tavera murmured, serving herself another bowl of soup. "Who we're after believes in the Goddess as well. So belief ain't exactly in our favor here, is it?"

Tender nodded, looking down. He drummed his fingers against the table top, as if waiting for someone to say something else. Tavera just sat and ate, nodding to Gaela as she started to eat as well. Eventually Tender sighed.

"Alright. You should come with us." The look on his face was one of surrender, but also relief. "Another body in this situation, willing and able, who can hold their own--"

"Probably better than you can," Little said.

"We don't know that for a fact!" Tender said. "Everyone here is capable of helping in some way and willing, and that is what the Goddess will honor. Our desire to help. Our desire to get Sister Kella back and out of harm's way. She will guide us through this, She will get us there safely and back safely and those who are wrong will be dealt with, as She deems."

Tavera blinked. It was the first time anyone had said anything about what was to be done with the cultists, with Cyric and his people. It was vague enough that Tavera didn't think now was the time to inquire further but it was something Tender had thought about, obviously. Tender looked to Tavera. "You vouch for her?"

"I'm not vouching for anyone," Tavera said. "I vouch for myself, and if that's good enough for everyone here, I'll take the same from them." She finished her soup and looked at the rest of the food, wanting to eat more but no longer feeling hungry. "We think we can do it, right? Right?"

"Yes," Tender said. Little nodded, his face serious.

"Yes," Gaela said. They sat there for a moment, picking at the food awkwardly. Gaela finally drew in a breath and spoke, breaking the silence. "So, when are we leaving?"

"First light tomorrow," Tender said. Tavera groaned inwardly. First light. Why did the days always start at first light? "Meet us here with anything you might need. The church is supplying food, horses, water, rain-cloaks."

"I don't have much," Gaela said with a smile. "Just clothes and some tools."

"Can you ride a horse?" Tender asked.

"Not...really, no," Gaela said sheepishly.

"She can ride with me," Tavera offered. She saw Little start to say something and then stop himself, blushing. "I'm not too sure in the saddle."

"She should ride with the best rider not the worst," Little said, matter-of-factly. "Can't risk losing the both of you because you can't keep your hands on the reins."

"He has a point," Tender said. "Sorry, Point, you'll have to ride your horse alone."

"It's fine," Tavera said, ripping into a piece of bread. "I'll manage. Or die from a horse-related injury."

"Are they dangerous?" Gaela asked.

"Only if you don't know what you're doing and even then, yes," Little said. His attempt at a joke failed. Gaela's face grew pale and Tavera had to laugh.

"Don't worry, Gaela," Tavera said. "Little's a good rider. And I'm sure the church will give us calm animals."

"I hope so," Gaela said with a smile. "Well, I should be going, I must prepare for tomorrow."

"Actually, will you stay a bit longer?" Tender asked, getting up from his seat. "We've a meeting with Sister Cera after vespers about what we've found out. Point, you can share what you know so we can make our plan before we leave." He picked up the plates in a stack, clearing the table without being asked. "Can you stay for vespers?"

"I can," Gaela said. "Will you all be attending?"

"I was going to step out," Little stammered. The brothers exchanged a look, Tender looking exasperated, Little quietly defiant. "I've things to get ready."

"If you just stay for vespers, you can do it after the meeting," Tender sighed, gesturing with plates still in his hands. "We can meet right after, then you can go do whatever it is you have to do. Please, just stay."

"Fine," Little said. "I'll stay."

"Good, it's settled," Tender said, a hint of triumph in his voice. "Temple, then a meeting with Sister Cera. She's been a great help to us." Tender didn't look at Tavera when he said it, but turned and walked toward the door leading to the main dining hall.

"Well, we've got a few breaths, I'm going to get washed up and changed before temple," Tavera said. "Gaela, want to stay here or come with me?"

"I'll stay here," Gaela said, looking around the room for the first time since they had walked in, eyes big. She looked to Little. "Make sure he doesn't run away."

"I'm sure his brother will appreciate that," Tavera grinned, picking up her pack. "Save me a seat?" she said, slinging it over her shoulder. Little nodded with a roll of his eyes and Tavera left, turning away from the kitchen and down toward the stairs leading down to the basement of the temple. Tavera waved at the priestess sitting at the top of the stairs who let her pass, her boots clunking down the stairs just as they had down so many church basement steps. A clean-shaven man came up the stairs, smelling of herbs and hair oil. Tavera wondered if he was going to temple or to meet someone. Under other circumstances, she might have tried to find out, but duty and Tender called.

Tavera snorted as she set her pack down on the hard floor, all the sleeping mats piled up for later use. A woman was using the wash bowl and pitcher so Tavera took off her cloak and looked through her pack for something to wear to temple. Her skirt was fairly unwrinkled. She yanked this out and pulled off her boots and britches, pulling the skirt on and tying it at the waist. She secured her belt around her hips, making sure her tunic covered it, and retightened the cords at the bottom of her underbust. Her cloak was traded for her shawl, a gift from Old Gam, the telltale embroidery almost like a signature.

Tavera couldn't help but hold it up to her face and inhale its scent. It had been a gift from Gam, and Gam always wrapped her gifts around a bundle of sleepsweet before she handed them over, scenting them. Derk had kept a good handful of herbs for his pipe in the shawl. When Gam had given it toTavera it had been too cold to wear it. She could still smell the tobacco and sleepsweet; it reminded her of

Derk giving Gam a kiss and Gam making a face after. Tavera held the soft fabric in her hands, tears starting to sting in her eyes.

A tap on her shoulder sent Tavera wheeling around, her mouth falling open, surprise on her face. Tender took a step back, almost as surprised as she was. "Sorry, didn't mean to startle you," he said. "I just, uh…I came down to get washed up, I saw you there but you didn't stir when I said your name." He put his hands on his back and rocked back and forth on his heels. "You okay?"

"Yeah," Tavera said. She sniffed and blinked, pushing her tears back as she draped her shawl around her shoulders. "Just got lost in thought," she managed, smiling and raising her brows at Tender.

"Right," Tender said. "Lots to think about." He looked off to the side while Tavera pulled her rosary out of her pouch, wrapping it around her wrist, murmuring the blessing over it.

"I'll see you in temple," Tavera said, ignoring Tender as he looked at her, walking over to the wash bowl. She heard him changing his shirt, pulling his old one off and putting a fresh one on while she splashed the water on her face, washing her hands in the clear water. She looked back to see him combing his hair with his fingers, feeling along his scalp to part his dark hair in the right direction. "You not gonna shave?" she asked.

"Nah," Tender said. "I look as serious as I feel with the beard." He smiled, his eyes squinting. Tavera wondered what he looked like without it but nodded.

"Fair enough," she said, drying her hands on the towel left by the priestesses. "See you," she said, ducking to the stairs and skipping up. As she walked the scent of her shawl went with her, mixing with the smell of the temple incense and candles till finally she was in the temple itself, the oil and perfumes of the altar drowning out her thoughts and old memories. Tavera slipped into a pew, staring up at the statue of the Goddess placed at the head of the temple, Her Black Hands outstretched in a gesture of acceptance. Tavera hoped the comfort of the Goddess was with Sister Kella, alone but surrounded. Before anyone else showed up, Tavera bent her head in prayer, hoping the four of them could do what they set out to do.

Chapter 12
Pasts Uncovered

Sister Cera closed the door, two other priestesses present in the room. Tavera recognized them from vespers, one of them older than Sister Cera. She had played the guitar during the singing, her alto voice lending itself prettily to The Valley is Her Love.

"This is Sister Mereel and Sster Perla," Sister Cera said. "They'll be getting your provisions ready for your journey." She looked to Gaela and smiled warmly. "I do not believe we have met."

"I'm Gaela," Gaela said. "I was apprenticed to the map maker but when I heard of Point and her friends' endeavors, I felt I had to come along."

"Those who are moved, the Goddess shall make a way for them," Sister Cera said. "I'm sure Berden appreciates you going when he could not."

Gaela simply nodded. She and Little sat at the table. In the service Gaela had seemed interested, curious. Little on the other hand...he obviously didn't want to be there. And Tender obviously didn't care about how

Little felt. Tender put a small stack of books between them.

"Well, we thank you for any help you can give," Tender said. Tavera knew something about the situation annoyed Tender but they didn't have the luxury of time for him to sort it out. Tender opened one of the books. "This is the account by the High Priestess who was here when Sister Kella was taken all those years ago. It mentions those who brought her back and it mentions the cultists numbered around forty-five. The party that went on the mission had two archers and a tracker with dogs. They subdued more than half of the cultists, sneaking up on them during a service. They found a dozen hiding in a room, door barred. The frail, women with child, children, the elderly. They found Kella by herself in a room, holding a sickle."

"What happened to the people they found who were hiding?" Little asked.

"All of them were asked if they wished to come to the Valley proper or remain in the Freewild," Sister Cera said.

Tavera frowned. "People who abduct people, asked to come into the Valley by the church?"

"Not the church," Sister Cera said. "The rescue party. They worked independently of the church and the barons, though we did provide them with food and gear.

"Where are those who came to the Valley?" Tavera asked. "Did they come back with Kella and them who rescued her?"

"They came back and were dispersed," Sister Cera said with a nod.

"Did you find anything about the magic?" Tavera asked, standing up.

"Magic?" Sister Cera said, her thin brows knitting together on her face. "What magic?" She looked to Tender.

"When Cy came to our town and left," Tender said. His face looked pinched, as if he hadn't wanted to bring it up. "It looked like the roofs were on fire but after a while the flames went out suddenly. Not a thatch had been burned."

"And," Tavera added, not able to keep from narrowing her eyes at Tender, "with the sickle. We exchanged blows from afar. I hit him with a dagger, he...his sickle started to catch light on it, and it shot at me. And...it hurt." Tavera held her breath, hoping no one looked at her like she was crazy. "He knocked me out and I had a strange dream. It felt real, very real."

"What was in the dream?" the sister asked. One of the other priestesses came forward and started searching among the books.

"It was all very familiar, but off," Tavera said. "It was a situation I had been in before, but...I'd been scared when it happened in real life. In my dream I was terrified."

"When she woke up, her eyes were covered in blood," Tender added, his voice low. "We thought she had a sleep-death on her but she woke up, thank the Goddess."

"What was that?" Tavera asked. "How can we protect ourselves against such things?" Tavera remembered the feel of the dream, her fear, Derk's ragged face and his hands at her throat. The feeling of her chest trying to force her to breathe but being unable to draw breath. The flash of the knife.

"I unfortunately don't know much about...I don't even know what to call it," Sister Cera said.

"It's old workings," Sister Perla said, leaving the book-shelves to address the small party. "Harking back to the days when many were imbued with Her Power, blessed or cursed, though far fewer were cursed." Sister Perla paused for a moment. "Those who had the power often bestowed a

part of it on objects to relieve themselves of the burden."
The older priestess watched them all, as if trying to gauge
their reaction. "It is not common and rarely used. Using
Her Power for the means of Valleyfolk is frowned upon by
the church. When such items are found, they're generally
confiscated."

"What if it's not the sickle itself?" Gaela asked. "What if
it was the man? Or some combination?"

"Only Wielders can generate power," Sister Perla said.
"The man is no Wielder, I can assure you. If he is a summoner, a pact maker...well, from what I've heard, their
methods are different, more physical. From the description
of the power and from what is known about the cult, it is
mystical. They commonly using trances and blood-letting
to induce states where they will be closer to their Goddess, the Goddess Bloodied. She who has been avenged
upon, who will avenge those who ask. The Goddess
Purged, who shall drain all iniquity from those willing to
pay the price."

"What...what do they want the plate for?" Tender asked.

"It is for one of their rituals," Sister Perla said. "Their
highest ritual. When the Avatar comes. Their version of the
Goddess pours herself into a vessel, to lead them to a new
place of power."

"Is this going to happen?" Little asked. "Is...this vessel...
not the plate?"

"The plate is needed to perform the ritual," Sister Perla
said. "The vessel is a child born at a certain time." Tavera
thought the sister was leaving something out. She thought
back to what she had read in Sister Kella's journals.

"Doctrine teaches us the time of flesh and blood believ-
ers taking on the mantles of the Goddess is in the past,
Herix," Sister Cera said. "The Goddess in Her power and

mercy no longer touches the souls and flesh of Her follow-ers. She gently guides through signs and good teaching."

"Well, someone should tell Cy and his lot that," Tavera said. "I don't think they're on the same liturgical calendar as us."

"What happens if they think they've succeeded?" Tender said. "What if they get their…Avatar?"

"They mustn't be allowed to think so, or they will con-tinue to terrorize those who cross their path," Sister Perla said. "They will abduct more people and recruit them to their cause. The Freewild will become a bloody place. They have grown bold to take Sister Kella and they will grow bolder under a new leader."

"Why did they take Sister Kella?" Tavera asked. "Why again?"

"My guess is because they think she knows where the plate is," Sister Perla said. "Luckily, you have found it and re-turned it to where it will be safe."

Returned the plate? The plate was in Tavera's bag.

"Do you think it could be because Sister Kella had a his-tory with them?" Tavera asked, trying not to sound an-noyed. "Maybe they think she should be there for whatever is about to happen. Do you think they consider her one of them? Her and Cy, they have…a history. He came himself to take her."

Sister Perla frowned. "Sister Kella does have history with the cult. And she worked closely with Cy. Her experience as a priestess is probably what drew him to her when he first abducted her. Sister Kella may have stayed, thinking her faith and learning would sway Cy over to the right aspect of the Goddess."

"I think she stayed there because she had to. She was afraid of them," Tavera spoke up. She had seen the journals,

the expression on Sister Kella's face. Cy was beyond reason-
ing with, it was obvious. "I think if the sister had thought
she could leave, she would have. And now she's back there."

"We hope you bring her back safely," Sister Cera said.

"We intend to," said Tender.

"Well," Tavera said, trying to smile through grit teeth.
"We should go to bed. Right? Must be up early in the morning."

"Your horses will be packed and ready to go," Sister Cera
said. "Again, thank you for rescuing Sister Kella. We are
thankful."

Little, Tender and Gaela stood, saying their goodbyes to
the priestesses before exiting. Tavera walked close to Tender, looking over her shoulder to make sure the priestesses
weren't following before she spoke.

"You gave them the bowl?" she asked, trying not to
sound angry.

"Of course I did," he said, surprised. "I told Cera I had it,
she said they should keep it, to be safe. Don't want to risk it
getting to the cultists, do we?"

"What're they going to do with it?" Tavera asked.

"Probably lock it up somewhere. Maybe sent it to Whitfield, I imagine."

"If they took it to Whitfield, that's the first place the
cultists would try to get it. It's too predictable," Little said.
"They'd probably send it to another temple. A small one."

Tavera placed her hand on the handrail and glared up at
Tender. "The bowl was in my saddlebag. You'd no right to
give it."

"The bowl isn't yours. The saddlebags were borrowed
from one of the people in Whitend," Tender reasoned.
"And what're you to do with it anyway? It's better the
church has it."

"Tender, speak with me outside, please?" she said. Tender just looked at her and then back to Little before Little and Gaela stepped to the side, giving them space to leave. Tavera went first, her heart thumping in her chest, her mind going over the details of the last meeting. They walked through the temple and through the side door, into the alley. Cool night air poured over her, the smell of another rain lilting on the breeze.

"Don't go through my bags," she said. "Just…don't. If my things are in them, don't look through them. If you want something, ask first. I think we should get that out of the way."

"Alright," Tender said. "Fair enough. In return, if you ever need anything from my bags, feel free to help yourself," he answered with a bit of a bow, trying to seem gracious.

"Secondly," Tavera said, ignoring the gesture. "Why did you give it to them? Without telling anyone?"

"You were out getting the map," Tender said. "We don't need the plate. The church will keep it safe."

"If the church can keep it safe, why did they have it hidden with Kella?" Tavera asked.

"Maybe because she…." Tender's voice trailed off. "Because they didn't know she had it?"

"Do you actually believe that? That she somehow smuggled it out of the cultists' temple, without her rescuers or the church finding it?" Tavera said flatly, rolling her eyes at Tender. "Kella had it because it was the last place the cultists would ever think to look." She waited for Tender to look at her. Instead he just stared at the floor, his previous smile fading with her words. "A temple basement, an archive, those are where they usually keep those sort of things. Not the run-down shacks of the worn-down priestesses who had to deal with them, in the Freewild. Yes, I know you've only been in the Freewild just since spring's start," she sighed, seeing Tender about to bring it up.

"But," Tender said finally. He sat down on one of the crates, hands together. He looked confused, the lamplight shining on his face. "This plate Kella held. It couldn't have possibly done her...any sort of good," he said, looking to Tavera. "Point, the pictures in her journal, what she must have gone through. To have a constant reminder of it in one's home, knowing who wants it. Why?"

Tavera sat down next to him, trying to puzzle it out. She thought back to the journals, the pictures of the other priestesses that filled the pages in the entries after her rescue. They must have rehabilitated her, retrained her in some way. "My guess?" Tavera said. "Maybe they thought it did her some good. All the time she had it, she could have gone to Cy and his lot and just handed it over and done all this again. But she didn't. Maybe knowing she didn't gave her something. Or," Tavera continued, not wanting to bring up the less hopeful possibility but feeling the need to. "Perhaps they were testing her. To make sure she wouldn't hand it over."

"She didn't," Tender said. "She never did." He sighed. "She had it this whole time and never told anyone."

"She kept her fear hidden," Tavera said with a shrug. "We give our fears to the Goddess."

"I'm afraid to do this," Tender said. He said it quietly, so quietly, staring ahead at the ground. "I'm afraid, Point. I... one of us might get hurt. Or killed. Or all of us."

"Some of us are already hurting," Tavera said. "And you don't only feel fear. You feel...anger, Tender. You feel... worry, for Kella. And us, who're going with you. You feel excitement, at the thought of succeeding. And zeal." Tender raised his head, the brave look he showed so readily back in his hometown starting to appear in his eyes once more. "You know it's wrong, what they've done. A crime against Kella and Our Lady. I heard what you yelled at Cy and I know the thought of them worshiping Our Goddess in this way, it disgusts you. You know the Goddess is good and full of mercy. Protecting, not causing harm."

Tender pulled his legs up and wrapped his arms around his shins, leaning his head back against the temple wall so he was staring up at the sky. Tavera sighed and put her hand on his face, offering him a smile. "Fear is natural, Tender. It ain't weakness. She don't laugh at our fears. She helps us through them." Tavera felt the heat of his skin on hers, the look in his eyes as he waited. She brushed his hair out of his face before mussing it a bit. He smiled at her, which was what she wanted. Tavera hopped off the crate.

"You going to bed?" Tender asked.

"Nah," Tavera said. "I've got to get the plate back," she said. Tender blinked and frowned, Tavera turning to head inside the temple.

"What?" Tender said. Tavera heard him hop off the crate and chase after her. "You're joking, right? You're not going to steal it."

"I'm getting it back," Tavera said. "We need it."

"Why?" Tender said in a harsh whisper. Tavera laughed at the guilty look on his face.

"We need it," Tavera said. "Cy laid it out very clearly, don't you recall? If we've no plate, we won't get Kella."

"But then they'll have it!" Tender exclaimed. "They can't have it! Sister Perla said!"

"And the map maker said we need to get Sister Kella back from them at any cost." Tavera turned around and faced Tender, looking him in the eye. "Would you leave her to them for a plate? Could you?"

"It's not just any plate, it's--"

"It's a piece of metal!" Tavera said. She looked around, realizing how close they were to the temple and hoping no one was listening. "It's well worked, it's pretty, people think it's important but it's a thing. It's not alive. Sister Kella still is."

"But Sister Perla said if the cultists have it, they can cause trouble with it. They need it for their ritual and if they succeed--"

"Do you think the Goddess will allow them to sully Her land with their stupid notions?" Tavera said. "That man will kill Sister Kella, I believe it. I know you believe it. And if they start trying to pick up people in the Freewild, people will avoid the area or send them packing."

"But--"

"I'll steal it back," Tavera said. Now Tender stopped talking. "We'll trade them the plate for Kella. Then we'll follow them back to their temple, sneak in and get it back." She turned and started to head toward the temple, her face feeling warm. "It's easier to smuggle a thing than a person. If you feel like hitting anyone on the head on the way out of their stupid temple, be my guest."

"But stealing is wrong!" Tender whispered.

"Kidnapping people and torturing them is more wrong," Tavera shot, turning to face him. Her words hit Tender so he winced. Tavera sighed, knowing he wouldn't argue anymore "Now, unless you have a plan which don't involve getting the plate back, I'd appreciate you telling me where it is and then, maybe…I don't know, distracting the priestesses. That'd be good."

"I'll…I'll see what I can do." Tavera and Tender regarded each other for a few breaths. Something in the way he said it told Tavera he'd do it. Tavera smiled and started to turn away. Tender grabbed hold of her arm. "It's in the High Priestess' room," he whispered.

"Oh," Tavera said, trying not to sound concerned. Her room? "Okay. I'll get it then, before she even notices it's gone. Easy, considering she isn't even here." She slipped into the shadows of the temple, leaving Tender with a worried expression on his face.

Chapter 13
Getting A Hold

Tavera tried to remember the looming structure of the temple grounds. The main temple faced east, as all temples did. Behind it was the courtyard, where she stood now. Stables were to the south, living quarters to the west, workrooms and storerooms to the north, as well as a garden. The temple had multiple entrances, as was custom, with the back entrance the quickest way to the basement where they were staying.

The priestesses, including the High Priestess, were housed in a different building altogether. There were rooms in the upper floors of the temple but these were used for group studies, smaller services and counseling. Each priestess would have a bed and trunk in the house to the west, toward the setting moon.

Tavera stood before this building. The High Priestess' room would be on the top floor. She'd have the biggest room. From the street, it would probably have a large, round window. On this side it had several smaller windows. Were they locked? Tavera sniffled, feeling the rain on the wind.

The shadows stretched through the courtyard. Tavera drew closer to the building while trying to watch her feet. Could the building be scaled? It was at least five men high and she'd heard terrible and hilarious stories of people trying to sneak up and down from the tops of buildings, only to be discovered in laughable or less-than-alive situations. She looked down at her boots. Not the best for climbing. Lights still shone in several of the windows. Tavera grit her teeth and walked around the building to the front.

"Is Sister Cera in?" Tavera asked the priestess at the door, an older woman whose hair was completely covered by her headscarf, neatly tucked in even at this time of evening. The older priestess smiled at her.

"You're with Tender, aren't you?" she asked. "Surprised you're not at the prayer he called for you all."

"They're for the Goddess' ears, not mine," Tavera said, bringing a smile to the woman's face. "So," Tavera continued. "Is Sister Cera here? I was hoping to speak to her about a...personal matter."

"I think she would be at the prayer," the priestess said. "You can go up and wait for her, if you like."

"Thank you, I think I will," Tavera smiled. "Which room is hers?"

"Second floor, third down on the left," the priestess said. "Her room should be open."

"Thanks," Tavera said, hoping the priestess' words indicated all the doors were open. It was one of the nice things about temples, Tavera thought to herself as she clipped up the stairs, her boots skidding across the wood. People didn't steal from priestesses, so no one watched for people to steal from them. Temples were occasionally broken into and Tavera knew church libraries were sometimes taken from but for most Valleyfolk, temples were off limits. Tavera told herself she wasn't stealing from the temple, just replacing an item they needed for the trip without bothering anyone. Sister Perla would probably be against her plan, decent as it was. But Sister Perla was a priestess. Tavera was Tavera. It was the sister's job to worry about holy matters and artifacts. It was Tavera's to sort this out with the least amount of bloodshed possible.

Tavera reached the door and stood there for a moment, making sure none of the doors she had passed were opened. Only the crackle of oil lamps could be heard in the hall, dark wood inlaid with white stone spanning before her. Tavera counted the doors on the floor. Five on each side. Ten rooms, half of the rooms probably being doubles. How many priestesses had Tavera counted milling about the temple complex? Fifteen sounded about right, including the woman at the door and the absent High Priestess. Tavera smelled cakes and berries being fried, meaning those priestesses were probably fixing a late supper for weary travelers or getting a head start on tomorrow's breakfast.

The stairs for the third floor were right by the other landing, and Tavera walked back the way she had come, quietly, listening for the priestess downstairs or anyone approaching. Boards under her feet bent but didn't creak as she stepped lightly up the stairs, reaching the third floor. A window at the far end of the hall let in a bit of light, lacy curtains billowing as the moonglow spilled across the floor.

Tavera saw one wall with two doors, one door on the opposite wall. Tavera thought this would be the High Priestess' room. She listened, satisfied with the lack of sound on the floor. As she crept towards her target she pulled her lock-picking tools out of sleeve, feeling their thin, cold familiarity. Boards creaking here didn't bother her as much. The woman downstairs probably wouldn't hear them, or would maybe think it was the building settling down for the night. Tavera wrapped her hand around the doorknob and tried it, finding it unyielding. Locked? She smirked.

With a look over her shoulder which was more force of habit than anything else, Tavera knelt and inserted the lock picks, wiggling them up and down to feel the pins in the cylinder yield to the metal fingers. Tavera listened and tried to feel it out, turning and hearing the lock give with a satis- fying 'pop.' A grin spread across her face and she gave an- other glance down the hallway before she pushed the door open and slipped into the room.

Tavera entered a large, airy space, the scents of the town below and the church compound around her mingling with the roomy accents of sheets and wooden furniture. A door- way led to what Tavera guessed was the bedroom. Tavera felt curious as to what kind of bed a High Priestess had but the object of her desire was before her. The plate was on the table, waiting for her. It wasn't in the saddlebag, as Tavera had hoped. She sighed and looked around the room for something to wrap up the bowl.

Nothing much. Tavera saw a table with two chairs, a ta- ble for food service with a pitcher and bowl for washing up and several bookshelves. Paintings hung on the wall and a statue of the Goddess, about two hands high, sat on a shelf above the large round window overlooking the town.

The town? Tavera huffed, looking out the window. A lit- tle obvious? Perking up an ear, she went to the bedroom to see if there was something in there she could use.

Tavera turned the knob and pushed, walking into the door as it budged slightly, and then stopped short. Some- thing was in front of the door. Another push and a shove re- vealed a room in complete disorder. Tavera's mouth fell open and then curled into a grin as she looked over the chaos of the room. Scarves, shawls, skirts and sheets all lay in heaps and piles on the single sleeper bed and on the floor, draped over the chair. Bed sheets lay half pulled out of a dresser.

"That'll do," Tavera mused, stepping over various garments and objects. She tried not to step on anything, so as not to leave telltale footprints but felt cloth of various layers under her feet. A bed sheet was quickly yanked from the drawer, other linens spilling out of the drawer when she tugged, taking the sheet to the front room to wrap up the plate.

Up close, touching it, a shiver ran down her spine. The tarnished silver attested to its age. Pieces of deep-red stone were embedded along the rim. In the center of the plate she saw two hands, holding what Tavera knew to be an anatomically correct heart. Tavera spread the sheet out before placing the plate squarely in the middle, wrapping it up and securing the sheet around the plate with several careful knots before she carried it back to the bedroom.

The window in the bedroom faced away from the street. It was small but less likely to have someone staring up at it. Tavera climbed up on the bed and opened the window, glad to find it well oiled. Below the window was a balcony for the apartment below the High Priestess. "Tits," Tavera muttered, thinking over her plan. She'd have to throw the plate farther out to get it to land safely and the window wasn't exactly large.

Tavera listened to make sure no one was out on the balcony before she gripped the plate as best she could, lobbing it gently toward the ground so it would fall on its bottom. With a rustle of branches and leaves. It landed in the bushes. Content it was safe, Tavera closed the window. She stepped over the clothes and shut the bedroom door behind her, making sure the front room was as she had found it. Perking up her ear, she listened at the front door before she eased out, locking it securely before she walked calmly down the hall and down the stairs.

Sounds from the lower landing told Tavera several priestess had returned and she peeked down the hall to see if any of the doors were open. One was cracked, but just a nudge. Tavera took a quiet breath before walking past the door, quickening her speed once she had cleared it and slowing down once she got to the top of the stairs.

"Not staying for Cera?" the old priestess said, raising a brow. Tavera walked by her, shaking her head.

"No, I found my answer while I waited," Tavera said, walking backwards, her eyes pulled toward the plate.

"Ah, the Goddess often does that, doesn't she! Well, I'll tell her you were by," the priestess said, waving.

"No need!" Tavera called. "I wouldn't want to trouble her. Thank you for offering." Before the priestess could say anything. Tavera broke away and headed down the narrow street, looking around before she hopped over the fence and approached the bushes.

The bushes were higher off the ground than she had thought. "Tits," Tavera cursed, looking around to make sure no one was watching yet again. She took a deep breath before she wiggled her fingers, trying to part the thick, leafy branches to give her a clear grab. The branches were strong. Twigs scraped at her face and she smelled the green scent of crushed leaves as she reached and clawed at the air, trying to get a hold of the bit of fabric hanging down. Her face grew hot. What would Derk say if he saw his girl, fighting with a bush for a score? He'd probably laugh. Tavera stifled a chuckle as she bent at the knees, jumping up and grabbing a hold of the parcel, yanking it towards her, a shower of pale green leaves spraying her.

She had the plate. Tavera would make sure it wasn't ruined later. She hopped back over the wall and walked down the street, the lanterns lit for the night. Tavera retraced her steps and wound up back at the map maker's building. A quick scan of the road got Tavera two small stones which she quickly threw up at the window, the glass rapping with the sound. A light grew brighter within the room and then the window swung open, Gaela popped her head out, confusion on her face.

"Point?" she said. "What is it?"

"Come down here," Tavera called.

"What for?" Gaela asked. There were people on the street, though several blocks down. Tavera sighed.

"Just come down, it's important! Tits," she muttered, walking to the building and leaning against it. After a few breaths she heard someone within, saw the light coming to the door. The lock clicked open and the door creaked, Tavera darting in before Gaela could walk out. "Hey, I need you to hold this."

"What is it?" Gaela asked. Tavera noticed her red eyes and wondered if she had been sleeping. If so, she'd woken up easily enough.

"It's something for the trip but I can't carry it. If you would hold onto it and bring it with you tomorrow, I'd ap-preciate it." Tavera smiled in what she hoped was an assur-ing way at Gaela. "Secret weapon, if you will."

Gaela narrowed her eyes at Tavera but held out her hand. "It's probably better I don't know, right?" Gaela said with a laugh.

"Now you've got it," Tavera said. "You catch on quick."

"In my line of work, I hear more than you might think," Gaela said with a yawn. "I imagine...nothing, I'm going to try to get back to sleep," Gaela said, shooing Tavera away with a wave of her hand.

"Right," Tavera said. "Lock up after me," she said. Gaela nodded, following after Tavera wearily. Tavera left, hearing the door lock behind her and she looked up and down the street before she stepped down into it.

Tavera hummed to herself as she walked back toward the temple thinking about what she had just done. She'd told Tender she was just getting something back but she had broken into a High Priestess' room. If she had been caught, what would have happened? Tavera would have lied about it. Tender would have vouched for her, right? If caught, would she have stayed?

She thought about how far of a jump it would have been from the High Priestess' room to the balcony. She could have made it, to the balcony and then down to the ground. Easily. All her stuff was back at the temple so an escape would have been a 'naked' escape, as some called it. Not the most desired event, but if it had to be done. Granted, the priestesses knew who she was, in a fashion. Saw her. People knew her name. Tavera sighed, wondering how this was going to turn on her.

Would Tender turn her in? She was certain he wouldn't for this. He was an accomplice of sorts, just as guilty. Not that she would rope him into it if it came to it. She couldn't. He'd allowed Tavera to steal the plate back because she had convinced him it had to be done and she couldn't think of another way to rescue Kella without it. Not in any plan she was involved with. Four people against more than a few handfuls? Cunning was needed more than brute force. She tended to think it was the answer for most situations.

Tavera turned around the corner and stopped short. In the middle of the courtyard sat Tender and Sister Cera, sit-

ting on one of the benches. The sister said something and
Tavera's good ear perked up, hearing Tender laugh. They
were both laughing and eyeing each other. Tender reached
up and put his hand on Sister Cera's face, but she leaned in
and kissed him first. Tavera watched. It seemed like a kiss
that had waited too long to happen drawing them closer to
each other. Their hands strayed over each other, their em-
brace growing hungry. Tavera finally narrowed her eyes and
tried not to watch, feeling her cheeks grow warm. Satisfied
they were too involved with each other to pay attention, she
walked through the courtyard, skirting the trees partially
hiding them from the other buildings, finally stepping
squarely into the path leading up to the back of the temple.

"Point!" Tavera heard Tender call her just as she was in
the doorway. She heard Tender say something to Cera before he called again, "Point!" Tavera just lifted her hand in
acknowledgment, not bothering to turn around. She simply nodded at the priestess who guarded the inside of the
door and walked down the hall, down the stairs to the
basement.

Little was already asleep, his blond hair managing to
look even more unkempt. Tavera saw only one other person
sleeping in the room and she sighed as she pulled off her
boots, setting them by the wall before she went to make her
bed.

Bedroll and blanket set up, Tavera stripped down to her
tunic, feeling very tired all of a sudden. Usually after a take
she was happy, excited. Now she couldn't manage a smile.
Tender. She went to the basin and pitcher provided, washing her hands and face before crawling into her bed set beside Little, the quiet of the basement room engulfing her.

Someone stirring woke her up and Tavera opened her
eyes. Whoever it was coughed and she knew it was Tender,

finally coming down. Tavera stiffened under her blankets, hoping he wouldn't notice and know she was awake.

"Point," Tender whispered. She heard him kneel beside her, felt his hand on her arm through the blankets. "You awake?"

"Tits, I am now," she lied, turning over. Tavera pulled her blankets up, covering as much of her body as possible. "What d'you want? We've an early day tomorrow."

"Did you get it?" he asked. A slight smile tugged at the corners of his mouth. Tavera narrowed her eyes, amused by how pleased he looked.

"Yes," she said flatly, rolling over. For a moment she thought he would leave her alone. But Tavera smirked into her pillow. "That was smart, the prayer service," she whispered.

"I would have asked for one anyway," Tender said. She listened as he set up his bed and washed, getting undressed. The sound of blankets and Tender sighing told her he had settled in. All she heard was their breathing in the room, though questions sounded in her brain. She wondered how long she'd been asleep. She wondered how long Tender had spent with Sister Cera.

"Well. Good night," Tavera said quietly. Now wasn't the time to ask. Now wasn't the time to care.

"Night," Tender yawned, rolling over in his bed, his back toward Tavera. She lay in her bed, wondering what would happen tomorrow. Perhaps Cera had given Tender the last kiss he'd ever get. Who was the last man Tavera had kissed? That stranger from her initiation. She groaned inwardly. She didn't even know his name. Tavera buried her face in her blankets and closed her eyes.

Her thoughts strayed to the man who had taken her back to his room, his dark hair, the scars embedded in his skin, his mouth on hers. Abruptly her thoughts turned to Sister Kella, wherever she was, alone and unloved. All of Tavera's weariness sped from her mind as she thought of Kella and Tender and herself, never being loved again. Tomorrow they would try to do something about this and Tavera would have to do all in her power to make sure they all came back.

Chapter 14
Plans Gone Awry

The bar was noisy and smoky, the pungent smell of many liquors and many drinkers washing over her as she walked in. The sounds of glasses, drunks and chairs scraping against the floor were comforting as she allowed them to envelop her. There was a fight breaking out in the corner but from the looks of it, it would end quickly and badly for the bald man. Women in too-tight bodices walked around with tankards in their hands. One with curly blonde hair approached her.

"Get you a drink, boy? A bit more than a drink?" the woman asked. Tavera pulled back her hat to reveal her feminine features and sly grin, and the woman smirked.

"I'll get what I want from the keep," Tavera said loudly, her voice muffled by the rowdy bar.

"Just as well, you ain't my type," the woman said and bustled off into the crowds, leaving the thief to her business.

"What'll it be, stranger?" The ugly barkeep had the features of a man who had been punched in the face too many times and the bearing of someone who had returned the favor all too often. Deep set eyes peered out from his leathery face and his thinning hair was combed over the top of his head, as if it would hide his sweaty skull. He fixed his beady gaze on her greedily, pulling out a clay tankard before she even opened her mouth to order. This was definitely the man. Gaela's charts had taken them in the right direction and several shaken Freewilders told them about the barkeep who dealt with the strangers covered in scars, who preached about a strange version of the Goddess. "Something strange, to be sure." Tavera pulled a bundle off her back, its bulk and awkwardness quickly tucked between her feet, wrapping the shoulder straps around her ankles as an extra precaution against someone taking it. The barkeep gave her a quizzical look. Tavera returned it with a confident smile, rapping her knuckles on the worn and nicked bar top. "I was told you could connect me with some people who might be interested in something I am selling."

The barkeep snorted, looking toward the door as it opened, a large bell ringing against the din when anyone entered. He shook his head and looked at Tavera, his thin lips disappearing as he pressed them together. "I don't know who told you that. Are you going to order or not?" He was obviously agitated by her question, probably asked the same thing multiple times a day, if he was who Tavera had been told he was. His disapproval of her question only inspired her to press on. He was going to help her.

"I would like a bitter if you have it," she said, not able to keep from looking to the side as a crash sounded from where the fight had ended. The bald man groaned loudly, his moans of pain barely audible over the laughs of those who watched. Someone unceremoniously lifted him up and headed for the door. It was time to grab the barkeep's atten-tion. "It don't matter who told me, just what I have. I have to get rid of it by the full moon, or rather...I am told it is wanted by the Red Moon, Pense."

He stopped short, as if drawing in his breath. Tavera saw it. Pense pulled the pitcher off the shelf and tilted it to pour.

"So...you're the one who has brought it, eh?" The beer gurgled as it filled the glass. He pushed it toward her, leaning in close in the event the din was not loud enough to mangle their words. "I thought a man was to bring it."

"It shouldn't matter if a man or a woman has brought it, as long as they get their goods and I get my money." The barkeep's eyebrows raised slightly. Tavera wrinkled her nose at him. "What?"

"I just thought...I was told--"

"What, that someone was going to trade this plate for that woman?" Tavera laughed, taking a gulp of her drink, not bothering to wipe her face before she spoke. "I've no need for women, especially not drunks who aren't even valued by the robe wearers, who dump them in backwater towns. However, I do need money and they apparently need this plate. So," she said, taking another smaller gulp of her beer. "Tell them I want fifty fullies and a dagger."

"Fifty? You hem-chewin' brat, how--"

"Oi!" she hissed, grabbing him by the collar, knocking her drink over in the process. Tavera pretended her gaze would burn a hole in his skull if she concentrated hard enough. "I will take this tossin' plate to the church at Briers and they will buy it from me for whatever stupid purpose they have for it! Now you set this up! I'll meet them out back at two fingers till and they had better show up or I'm gone. And if I get gone, they won't get a hold of me or their fappin' piece of shit relic for a good long time." She let go of the barkeep, their scuffle apparently not drawing any attention from any of the other patrons. Tavera felt her sleeve grow cold and wet as she set her arm back down on the bar-top. She fixed her hat atop her head; it had fallen askew when she grabbed the man.

"I'll see what I can do." He sounded defeated, as if her demands had trampled him down and he was having a hard time getting back up. For a second she considered pitying him, but he was a middle man, someone who preyed off of people desperate to get rid of things and acquire things. By the few accounts they gathered, he was mostly retired, but there were always a few things he couldn't turn down and a few parties he couldn't say no to. The Temple of the Red Moon Rising had not yet ripped their claws from his flesh.

Something bothered her, though. Something in the pit of her stomach told her that there was a piece of the puzzle she had missed. The situation felt off. Was it with Pense? Or was it with the picture as a whole?

"And get me another drink, damn you," she muttered, keeping her eyes fixed on him. Did he know something she didn't? He had to. He dealt with the cult on a somewhat regular basis and supposedly, Cy and a few others even visited this bar on occasion. Barkeeps knew people and if they trusted him with important arrangements as well as a way to get a hold of them, he could know some very important things indeed.

The beer sloshed out as he set it firmly on the bar top, obviously annoyed with her, glaring at her. It chilled her down to the bone, the way he looked at her, but Tavera managed to keep calm, sitting as still as a statue and meeting his gaze with an equal amount of energy.

"How'd you get the plate?" he asked, tilting his head to the side. So, he wanted information. His annoyance had been tempered by curiosity and she would satisfy it, in order to get her money.

"I stole it," she said simply. She wrapped her hands around the mug and took a long pull off of the drink, glad to have some good beer in her belly after a long day's travel. "I was in the village it was being kept in when the request was made. While the town was in a ruckus over the loss of their beloved priestess, I slipped in and found it." She shrugged. It didn't sound like something she wouldn't do. Had the circumstances been different, it was something she might have done.

"And you traveled alone? No one followed you?"

Tavera snorted. "Yes and yes. I'm by myself. The people in the town are too stupid to figure anything out. The only person who seemed capable of doing anything won't get far." She drained her cup, her stomach feeling warm as the liquor seemed to spread throughout her middle. They brewed strong beer in this bar. It would probably be best if she slowed down.

Tavera nodded, adjusting her hat again as she leaned back a bit in her chair. "One of them…zealous sort, the kind people don't talk to, if you catch me." The half-elf knew better than to have conversations when the drink was strong and so she slid off her seat, hoisting her pack and the well-hidden plate onto her back. She didn't bother finishing her drink but instead set the mug on the table and tied her cloak about her neck. "Look, I'm more interested in a game of cards than speaking to you. Get them to show up with my monies and a dagger or I might be willing to part with yet another one in a rather bloody fashion." The barkeep nodded, narrowing his one eye at her before taking her mug off the bar.

"Ain't you gonna pay for this?" he asked, looking down into the bottom of the mug, his face screwing up as he saw she hadn't drunk but a third of it. Tavera shook her head as she pulled her hood over her hat, the brim pushing forward so that she had to adjust it again.

"I only had a few sips, you can resell it, I suppose," she laughed. "I'm just giving you another reason to help me out!" If he called after her, she didn't hear it. Her heart thumped in her ears and even the extreme noise in the bar was drowned out by her working brain. Her legs felt wobbly, a combination of the strong drink and her nerves, she supposed. The moon was almost high, she told herself, stepping out into the spring rain. She wondered when she had last waterproofed her pack and couldn't remember. Tavera cursed under her breath, steam rising out of her mouth as she made her way to one of the other buildings that made up the small community of Black Hills. If it rained harder, her things might get wet. If it rained harder, any tracks the cult made might be washed out.

Details which could not be overlooked sprouted in her brain. Tavera sat down on the stoop of what looked to be an abandoned building, cataloging what had already happened and what was to come. She went over various scenarios in her head, making pathways of plans which branched out and crisscrossed, solutions and proposed reactions pointing all roads toward one goal: success. It was important not to entertain thoughts of failure but to plow toward the desired end, regardless of what obstacles placed themselves in her way. In their way.

Tavera took a deep breath, the urge to walk around suddenly seizing her. She pulled her cloak off, the cold air and water threatening to seep through to her skin as she hurried to get her pack back on, draping the cloak over it and herself. It made the fabric hang on her in an awkward way, but at least the journals which had helped them so much would fare better.

She was about to step off the porch when a figure walked around the corner of the house, the black cloak lined with red dragging on the ground. Tavera drew in her breath, the boots and cloak registering in her brain, dreading the face hiding within the hood. The scarred face of Cy stared back at her, his expression cold, though one eye glinted with what seemed to be amusement. Several other figures stepped out from around the house, all of them wearing the same robes. Their faces were harder to see but Tavera felt a chill run through her, knowing they were watching her.

"Well, you're early!" she said, unable to keep the nervousness out of the laughter she forced out of her mouth. Her mouth felt dry. The rainy mist made her squint. How long was it till the time she had given them? Would their tracks last long enough for Little to follow? Tavera rubbed the side of her face with her hand, scanning the area for a quick escape if needed. "Well this is lovely, we can make our trade and I can be on my way. Did Pense tell you about what I required?"

"Yes, he did, as a matter of fact." Cy's voice was low and measured, almost melodic in quality. And calm. Too calm. It made Tavera nervous. She struggled to hide it, push it down into her warm belly. Cy's eye twinkled despite the lack of light. "Fifty white pieces as well as...a dagger?" He tilted his head to the side slightly, seeming to peer down at her. Tavera gulped.

"Yeah, I seem to have misplaced one of mine in someone's shoulder just a few days ago. I do seem to lose more sharp things that way." Tavera spat the words, hoping she was convincing. She was no match for Cy and his friends, but they didn't need to know that. Tavera knew where she would run if he pointed that sickle at her. She wouldn't risk being knocked out again in Black Hills. That being the case, they had to believe she would stand her ground and send them to Her Hems if they didn't deliver.

"You seem to be misplacing a lot of things these days," Cy said. Someone was pushed out from behind the building, led at knifepoint by yet another cultist. A smile crawled across Cy's face as Tavera tried not to react, the thief biting her lip so hard she drew blood as she tried to keep herself from losing her semblance of control. Cy chuckled as he reached into his cloak. Pale, scarred fingers wrapped around the hilt of the dagger Tavera had attacked him with all those nights ago.

"How about this," Cy began. "Instead of trading the plate, which you don't need, for the priestess, who you don't need, I instead give you this dagger? Embedded in this bartender. Would that be more to your liking?"

The look on Tender's face made Tavera's heart threaten to rip out of her chest. She felt sick. A million apologies were painted across his face, his eye swollen where someone had apparently hit him. Tavera's legs felt as if they would melt beneath her but she drew in her breath, slow and measured. The sharp taste of blood in her mouth streamlined her thoughts to where they needed to be. Perhaps her original plan could yet be salvaged.

Tavera made a point to keep her eyes off of Tender and fixed them on Cy, not breaking her gaze as she gestured at the barkeep. "Do what you like with that fapper. Did you even bring any money?" Exasperation rang heavily in her voice, though money was the last thing on her mind. She had to get Tender out of this somehow. Her hands reached up, undoing the clasp keeping her cloak fastened, and she let it fall to the ground, swinging her pack around so she could get to the object they so desperately wanted. "I have the plate."

She held it up, the leather bag with the silver clasp obviously holding something large inside. Hopefully, the presence of their quarry would distract them long enough for Tavera to think of a plan. Indeed, the robed figures seemed to hone in on the sacred item, the hoods all turning, unspeaking. A flicker of excitement shone in the single eye of Cy, the cruel scar jerking as he drew in his breath.

"I could just kill the bar keep, take the plate from you and make you our prisoner," Cy finally said. He flipped the dagger in his hand, catching it with his opposite hand rather skillfully. He turned his eye toward Tavera. She knew for a fact she disliked the look he was giving her. "However," he continued. "In the short time we have come to know this barkeep, he has proven himself to be a very serious man. A very dedicated fellow. He is devoted to the Goddess in a way many men born in this time aren't." Cy flourished the dagger again before tucking it back in his belt, the folds of his robe falling into place as if they had never been disturbed. He didn't look to Tender as he spoke of him, but walked backward, taking a hold of the rope tied around his neck.

"I have found it is sometimes easier to transfer a fire from one fuel source to another, rather than ignite one anew." He yanked at the rope. Tender was caught off guard, lurching forward on his feet, stumbling. "I am so glad he followed you. This truly is an auspicious time for our people." Cyric folded his hands in front of him and finally, Tavera looked at Tender, the rain seeming to rise off of her like steam as her anger grew.

"Toss all this, just take your damned plate and leave me be!" A new plan formed in Tavera's head, a different one. She had looked over the journals. She had deciphered the pictures and she knew what they would do if they got their way, if they got both her and Tender back to their temple.

Tavera hadn't told Tender what they were capable of. Perhaps this had been her biggest mistake. He had been more concerned about her than himself and the fact this might result in him becoming a bloody, raving mess on the temple floor rankled more than any wound she might sustain in the fight she was about to start. Tender should have been more scared going into this mess and now Tavera fought to keep her fear from stopping her from acting.

"Just take the fapping plate and to Her Hems with you!" she shouted. Tavera spun on her heels, whipping the bag around by its thick straps, letting it go at just the right time. It hurtled toward Cy through the air in a wide arch. Tavera threw herself after it, pulling out her short sword as she shot toward him. Cy reached out for the bag, catching it, the bag covering his chest as he held it in his arms.

But there was a spot in the groin Derk had told her about. She aimed for it. The point of her sword sunk into flesh. It grated against bone as she twisted, not able to keep the low, animal growl from bubbling out of her throat and past her lips as her blade struck true. Her scream matched his as he stared back at her with his eye wide, his pupil dilated in shock and pain. She drove the blade in until he dropped the bundle, something slick and hot splashing onto her grip.

Everyone around her was shouting and Tender's voice seemed to be one of the many in the din. Tavera yanked, trying to rip her sword out of Cy's leg but it was stuck. Cy's pale hand rose from his side, his fingers clawing towards Tavera. A ball of light smashed over her forehead as he struck her with something which had no substance. Tavera's head snapped back from the blow. She found her joints loose and her muscles slack, her eyes unable to focus in her head. The thief felt annoyed as she slumped to the ground, the same shade of red creeping over her vision yet again.

Before everything disappeared, she saw them put a bag over Tender's head before someone picked her up off the ground. Tavera barely felt the rain as it washed over her and she dreaded the dreams which would come to her under the cultist's spell.

Chapter 15
Physical Escape

Tavera's mouth was dry. It was as if someone had poured salt into it while she had been sleeping. The sensation of her tongue being stuck to the roof of her mouth was about to make her gag. Tavera retched where she lay, working her mouth in an attempt to get her saliva flowing, trying to think of something good to eat. It usually worked.

A pitcher sat just a few feet away from her, a loaf of brown bread beside it. Her joints still ached. Nothing felt broken and she wasn't bound so she flipped over onto her belly, wincing as pain shot through her limbs She dragged herself toward the food, the cold, stone floor sucking her heat through her clothing. Tavera shivered as she reached out for the pitcher, managing to prop herself up on one arm to reach it.

"Don't drink it."

Tavera nearly screamed. Her mouth was too dry to even squeak. She sat up, her body trembling as her eyes made out the figure sitting on the straw mattress. The woman's face looked ashen, her eyes bloodshot.

Kella, the priestess. For a moment they just stared at each other in the dim cell. An oil lamp in the corner threw harsh shadows around the room. This was something like luck. Tavera had thought she would have to escape her own cell before finding the priestess. But here Sister Kella sat, staring at her. Her robes were dirty and stained with blood both old and new, but Tavera saw no wounds on her. She should assess the priestess' condition before she moved her. If she opened the door only to find the woman couldn't run or was in too much pain to move, her plan would be shot. Tavera stood up, grimacing as her own aches coursed through her.

"Wing?" said Sister Kella.

Tavera blinked as the priestess addressed her. Why had she just called her that? The priestess tilted her head to the side quizzically, the older woman's stare blank as she regarded Tavera. "Wing...when are we going to get out of here? When will they come rescue us?" Kella's voice sounded small, the older woman leaning forward with the question.

Tavera thought for a moment before she answered. "I...I am going to rescue us, Sister Kella," she managed, her voice sounding like gravel. Her throat burned as she spoke. She choked on her own words, taking a moment to catch her breath before she stepped toward the woman with her hands up. "But first...first I want to check you to make sure we can run for it. Is...is that okay?" The priestess stared at Tavera. It was starting to trouble her. There was no way the priestess could still be drunk, after all these days of solitude. Her peculiar alertness implied liquor was not the cause of the priestess' strange behavior. Tavera's thoughts turned to Kella's journals and her warning about the water. In her haste, Tavera had almost drunk it. Whatever was wrong with Sister Kella, she had at least thought to warn Tavera away from the drugged drink.

"Of course, my love." The priestess smiled as Tavera walked up and knelt before her. She looked over the priest-ess' feet, which were dirty but uninjured. Her ankles seemed fine; the priestess laughed as Tavera took each foot in her hand and tested them. As she inspected the woman's legs she spotted one of the causes of the bloodstained robe. All along her leg were small scars and scabs, some fresher than other. They had been made with a very sharp blade. Tavera reached for Sister Kella's hands, only to have the priestess grab her face. Startled, Tavera fought the urge to push her away, cringing as the priestess pressed her cheeks too hard.

"Wing, how did you get here? I'm sorry I wasn't able to help you, I couldn't. I wanted to, but...." The priestess' fin-gers brushed the tops of Tavera's ears and she drew her hands back, recoiling as Tavera sat up, staring back at the holy woman.

Sister Kella shook her head and put her hands on her face, rocking back and forth on the small mattress. "No, you're not Wing, you're not her. Wing is dead, Wing is dead, Wing is dead and I'm alone. Why did you do it, Wing? I'm sorry I wasn't as strong as you, I couldn't help it. I didn't know, I couldn't help you."

Tavera dared not move; instead, she tried to lick her lips, her skin cracking as she moved her mouth. It hurt and it bled but the scant bit of moisture seemed to do her tongue some good. Just when she was about to stand up, the priest-ess grabbed her by the arm, her eyes wild with emotion though her face was blank.

Tavera struggled against her hold, unable to shout. The strength in the crazed priestess' hands made Tavera wince. The thief could not risk getting injured by the priestess or no one would escape. With a twist and a shove, she man-aged to ram her knee into the Sister Kella's stomach, loosen-ing her manic grip enough for Tavera to slip from her grasp.

The older woman doubled over on the floor, clutching her gut as she moaned, her graying hair spilling over her face. Tavera backed up till the cool slickness of the cell wall pressed through the fabric of her clothes. She watched the woman, waiting to see what the priestess would do next.

Sister Kella looked up after what seemed like too long, her hand shaking as she brushed her limp, greasy hair out of her face. Though her breathing was rapid, her eyes seemed calmer and she fixed them on Tavera, licking her lips as she tried to sit up on the stone floor. "You're…you're Tender's girl, aren't you?"

Tavera snorted. She began unlacing her belt, plucking at the cords quickly before pulling the article off. Goosebumps crept over her skin but her fingers were able to pull at the stitching, undoing a few seams before she found what she had hidden there when she first obtained the garment. Two lock picks carved from bone were quickly pulled out of their sleeves and the garment tossed on and laced tight enough for the sake of convenience. There was another one sewn into the hem of her trousers, this one metal. With a few rips, the bit of wire was produced. Tavera held it in her hands, warming it up as she considered the priestess.

"I am not 'Tender's girl.' I'm someone who thinks you don't want to be here. I'm working with him, though." Ap-parently they hadn't changed the locks since last time Kella was here. Just like in the journals, they were locked with a key. The plate which kept the mechanism in place was held on with four screws. She had always been good at picking locks, better than Derk, which he had seemed to resent on occasion.

The thief listened carefully for the telltale signs of close company before she rapped lightly on the door with her knuckles, waiting for some kind of audible reaction. No one pulled back the peekhole and all she heard on the other side of the door was silence. The only noise came from her own, raspy breathing.

"They are getting ready for the ritual," the priestess said, her voice melodic. Tavera heard her approaching from behind. The thief hunched her shoulders instinctively. She had come to rescue Sister Kella but at the moment, she did not trust the priestess. Being here again had caused the woman's mind to break. It meant she would more than likely be a burden when they tried to escape. Tavera was bent on getting Tender out as well. There would be no leaving without him. She used the end of one of the bone picks to begin unscrewing the plate, finding the age of the metal giving her a rough start but not making it impossible.

"You are probably correct," Tavera said quietly, undoing the first screw and letting it fall to the ground with a satisfying metallic thump, the object bouncing across the floor before it made a few lazy circles and stopped. The thief would try to feel the priestess out and direct her thoughts to more pleasant matters. After all, Tavera had read her journals. She knew what Sister Kella had gone through and planned to use it to her advantage. Her mouth was still dry and her lip stung where it had cracked but she had to keep the priestess with her. "Tell me, did Tender say I was his woman?"

The priestess laughed and sat on the floor, picking up the loaf of bread with her hands. She set it on her lap and began picking it apart, tossing crumbs of it onto the floor. "They make the food for the prisoners so salty...but no, he never said that." The priestess looked up, her head bobbing gently, her dirty hands ripping through the crust. "But he spoke of you. Asked what I thought of you. He asked what I thought you were hiding." The priestess tucked a piece of the bread into her mouth, chewing it as a thoughtful expression came onto her face. "They poisoned the food."

"What?" Tavera looked over her shoulder briefly, still unscrewing the next screw as she gave the priestess a look, her voice incredulous. "Well then, why are you eating it?"

"They salt the bread and offer tea. The tea is poisoned. It turns your thoughts. It weakens your mind so they can re-build it." The priestess looked down at her lap, the folds of her robes full of crumbs. Her hands shook as she tried to brush them off, her eyes narrowing as she concentrated on the task. "It doesn't work on everyone, not everyone who drinks it can escape and be led back...I told him to stay away from you. You are one my husband would try to help. He would purge you of your secrets."

Husband? Tavera's pointed ear perked up. This time she turned to address the priestess. Her eyes narrowed as she tried to guess who the priestess was speaking of, pages of the journals flipping back and forth in her imagination as she tried to piece it together. They fell open to one page and Tavera's eyes lit up, a dark realization entering her thoughts. "Cy...Cy is your husband?"

The priestess nodded; her expression was a mixture of guilt and shame, her hands going up to her face to hide it. "Cyric...he is my husband." She sat up straighter, trying to give the impression of pride as she fixed her mussed hair. "That's why he came to get me. He wanted to be with me."

The thief took a deep breath. Tavera knew telling Sister Kella Cy was most likely dead was not the best idea at the moment. But there was no way the priestess believed what she had just said. Regardless of any vows they had taken years ago, Cy's intentions with Kella were nothing close to romantic. Tavera glanced at the pitcher of water, picking it up with one hand. With a flick of her wrist, she tossed the water into the priestess' face. The older woman squealed in discomfort and blinked her eyes. Before she recovered, Tavera grabbed her by the shoulders, shaking her to grab her attention and keep Kella in the moment brought to her by the wet and cold.

"Now listen to me, Sister. That ain't true." Tavera did her best to keep her voice sympathetic but strong, trying to lead the disturbed woman with her voice. "Cy kidnapped you. He was not kind to you. He took you from your home, where people depend on you, and brought you here, where they keep you in a cell. You hate it here. This place scares the shit out of you. Your friends died here. I know that and Tender knows that so we came here to come and get you… and take you home." Tavera moved the priestess' face with her hand as the woman tried to break her gaze, her gray eyes swimming with fear, but Tavera would not let her slip away again. "That is what you want, Kella? Right? Don't you want to be rescued?"

"I told him to stay away from you." The priestess looked down to the ground as tears fell from her eyes, her face pale. She sobbed softly. Tavera led her back to the bed to sit before she went back to work on the lock, looking over her shoulder occasionally to let the priestess know she was listening. "I knew if he started talking to you, he'd get ideas in his head. His eyes would look toward the roads and his scope would grow wider. Whitend would be too small." The priestess shook her head and pulled her hair back out of her face, hunched over so she looked like a shaking, gray blob. "You should not have come here to get me. You should have let me die."

"Well, you asked for Tender's help and you got it." Tavera snapped at the priestess, managing to get the last screw undone, prying the plate off with her fingers and setting it on the ground before she started in on the lock. "You called out to him for help. He came and now he's locked up some-where. Seeing as you're the only one who's been here before, I'm taking you with me to help me find him. When we've done that, I will gladly lock you back up so the cultists can bleed you and pray over you and prey on you, though I think it will irritate Tender since he came all this way to get you." There was a metallic clink as the metal pick finally caught and disengaged the lock, the feeling of the bolt sink-ing back into the door itself putting a smile on the thief's face. She tucked the tools behind her ear and stood up, feel-ing triumphant as she stood before the priestess. "Now, are you ready to come, or not?"

The priestess stared up at her from the bed, her eyes wide in disbelief. Slowly, the realization of escape seemed to dawn on her, her expression painted with a smile as she stood, walking over to Tavera, her hair still wet and stuck to her face. She laid a dry, rough hand on the half-elf's face.

"Thank you," she said, and for a moment Tavera thought perhaps the priestess thought she was someone else. But the woman's eyes refocused and she took Tavera's hands, earnestness in her words as she spoke. "I'm sorry I'm being like this, I really am. It's just very…difficult for me to be here. Before we go out, I must tell you something." The priestess' eyes shimmered and her breath was quick as if something pained her suddenly, her grip tightening on Tavera's hands. "I don't want to stay here, I want you to take me with you. Please, I can't stand…the memories. But there is another person trapped here, a girl, like I once was." The priestess started to say more but the tears forming in her eyes kept her from speaking. Tavera sensed the urgency and what the priestess asked was more important than their original plan. Before she begged, Tavera nodded her head, pressing her bleeding lips together.

"We will, but first we have to save Tender." The priestess began to protest but Tavera interrupted, putting a hand up to stop her. "I won't be able to get her by myself. We have people on the outside who are going to be with us soon, but I am going to need Tender's help to get this other girl. Do you understand?" The priestess nodded, smiling as Tavera released her. Placing her hand on the door, she pulled it open. She did a good job of hiding her relief as they stepped out of the cell and into the corridor. Tavera had told herself she could do it but actually doing it...she let a small sigh rush past her lips as she peeked around, motioning for the priestess to follow her.

Tender. The priestess took up the lead position, walking confidently down the corridors which were familiar to her. Tavera turned her thoughts toward releasing Tender, unsure as to what they would find and hoping they would be able to rescue him. Whatever the girl was in for, whatever the cultists thought they were going to do...they were in for a big surprise. What surprise? Tavera would figure that out when they got there.

Chapter 16
Loosed

"He's in here," Sister Kella whispered. Tavera nodded, looking around, straining her ears to listen for anyone who might be around and finding no indication anyone was close. Where she and the priestess had been trapped was underground, as most jails were. The halls seemed to slope upward and she felt as if they were midlevel, something over their heads. Probably the temple proper. One step at a time, she told herself, taking a deep breath.

Tavera peered through the window, her eyes taking some time to adjust to the lighting within. On the back wall, surrounded by illuminating lamps, was a grotesque image of the Goddess. Tavera saw the sacrificial victim depicted across her lap, the use of red paint, the left hand of the Goddess raised. In the center of her black palm was something red, what looked like blood dripping down the Goddess' pale arm. Tavera smelled strange incense, so similar to the kind used in temples, but different.

But where was Tender? The sister had said he was in there. Tavera listened to be sure they were alone in the hall again before she looked to Kella. "Are you sure?" she asked. Her lock-picks were already out.

"I'm sure," Sister Kella said. "He's in there."

Tavera thought to question Kella further but didn't. She took another glance and gasped, seeing what she hadn't before. Tender was on the floor. His hands and neck were in stocks, his back toward her as he lay awkwardly. Overturned chairs told her something had happened. Red blood ran in stripes on his bare arms. Was he breathing? Tavera rushed to unlock the door, fumbling at first but managing to get it open. She pulled it open enough for her and Kella to dart in before quickly locking it behind them.

"Tender," Tavera whispered as loudly as she dared. A hint of movement. He was breathing at least. She looked back at Sister Kella. The priestess' eyes were wide and focused on the mural, her body tense. "Sister, you stay by the door and listen," Tavera said, taking her by the shoulders and turning her away from the religious icon. "I'll make sure Tender's not hurt."

"Yes," the priestess said, her voice quavering. Tavera watched her for a breath to make sure Sister Kella wouldn't just turn around but the priestess faced the door. Tavera rushed carefully to Tender's side, stepping over broken pottery and the overturned chair.

"Braxton, what have they done to you," Tavera murmured. She squeezed beside him, easing him up into a sitting position. Tender groaned as she moved him and Tavera cursed, hoping she wasn't injuring him further. When he was sitting up, she looked to the door before grabbing one of the oil lamps and bringing it closer to him.

His face was covered in blood. Panic rose in Tavera's chest but she remembered Sister Kella's legs. She reached up and found a pitcher of what was probably the tea the priestess had warned her about. Tavera thought for a moment before ripping her shirt sleeve, soaking it in the tea before she wiped Tender's face. The blood came off readily. His eye was swollen but she carefully pried it open to make sure it was still there. Tender winced, groaning again but moving his head. She rinsed the rag and then dabbed again, seeing the crusted blood on the wounds made at the start of his scalp. His chest had been cut as well, blood smeared across his chest and belly. The incense was thick, making it hard to breath. "Tender," Tavera coughed. "Tender, it's me. I'm here to get you out."

"Mistress?" Tender muttered. He sounded as if his mouth was dry. "Have you heard my prayers?" His words were slurred. Tavera picked up the pitcher and stood, holding it over his head.

"I'm going to pour something over you, Tender. Try not to drink it," Tavera said. She waited for Tender to acknowledge what she had said. He just sat there, his mouth moving. She put a hand on the top of his head and poured the water over him, wiping his face with the rag, kneeling down to clean his chest and stomach. All cleaned up, his wounds weren't too bad.

"Can you move your legs?" she asked. Tender nodded, moving one foot and then the other. Tavera nodded, blowing out her cheeks, and she looked to the stocks. "Okay, I'll see about the stocks and then we'll be out of here, I promise."

"And then we'll get Point," Tender said. Tavera frowned. She pushed his dark hair out of his face, looking into his eyes.

"Braxton, it's me. I'm Point," she said. For a breath Tender just stared at her, his split lip wrinkling as he frowned.

"Holy Mother," he said. "It is you. Point. I--" He stopped short, cutting himself off. "I'm...I'm sorry. I didn't listen to you."

"It's fine, Braxton." Tavera looked to Sister Kella, the woman still staring at the door. "It worked out, in a way. I got the sister." She managed a smile, seeing Tender's face light up. "Now I just have to get you out of here."

"Can you do it?" Tender asked. "Can you deliver us?"

Tavera pressed her lips together, bringing the oil lamp closer to look at the hinge. "I can do lots of things, Tender. Mostly, I just try my hardest."

"I didn't believe you," Tender admitted. "I didn't think you could fend for yourself."

"To be fair, we are both in a jail cell," Tavera chuckled.

"I second-guessed you," Tender said. His dark, wet hair started to curl on his forehead. His eyes shone bloodshot in the dim light.

"You don't know me, Tender," Tavera murmured, turning her attention back to the lock. "Of course you did." She squinted in the low light, running her fingers over the hinge.

"Tits," she cursed, inspecting the way the stock was laid on him. The hinge was screwed into the wood. On the other side, a lock kept the two pieces together. Long metal pins were screwed into the wood between the spaces for his hands and head, securing the stock further. The metal rings which the easier lock was placed through was dented. Something had pushed the metal hard enough that it had bent. It would be difficult to pry even the easier lock out. "Tender," Tavera said. "Did you try to get this off yourself?"

"Yeah," Tender muttered. "Almost broke my own neck doing it."

"You're lucky you didn't," Tavera sighed. The stocks hinged at the end and two pins kept the wooden posts together. "What'd you bang this against?" she asked.

"The wall," Tender said. "And the floor I imagine, when I fell."

"It's dented." Tavera huffed. "I don't...." She shook her head, poking her finger in the hole where the pins went. "It's going to take a bit of doing."

"Do it, please," Tender said, grimacing. He gazed at her through half-lidded eyes, obviously straining where he lay. Tavera stood in front of him and took his hands, pulling him forward with a grunt, doing her best not to hurt him any more than she had to. The priestess prayed quietly in the doorway and Tavera forced a smile as she got working on the hinge.

She heard a distinct "clink" as the lock was picked. It popped open but wouldn't budge. Tavera wrapped her hand around it, trying to wiggle and ease the shackle without moving Tender too much. Metal scraped against metal as she pulled and jerked at the lock. With a final pull, she yanked the lock out of its ring. Tender winced as the stock shifted with the force, gritting his teeth. Tavera got over to the other side to start working on the other hinge.

"How...how do you know how to do this?" Tender asked.

"Do what, Tender?" she asked. She looked at his feet, bare and dirty. After she got him out she'd have to find his boots.

"This," he said. He moved his hands in the stocks, as if to gesture. "Undo locks. Talk to people like you did in the alley. And then like this, in this...this prison." His shoulders slumped.

"This...this is what I do, Tender," Tavera said. If she kept talking, it might cheer him up and keep him with her. She saw the knot on his head where someone had hit him. The back of his head was shiny in one spot, red. Fresh blood. Tavera noticed Tender's eyes fluttering toward the mural of the Goddess, terrible in its depiction. "Hey, don't look at that," she said. "You know it's a lie. That's the real lie here, Tender. You know the Goddess is good and not one to bring her children pain."

"Right," Tender said. He sounded like he believed it. Tavera let one of the screws fall to the ground and then hopped up, blocking the view of the mural. Tender moved his head in something like a nod while she gripped the hinge with her fingertips. The hinge was pried off of the stock, leaving only the two long screws to deal with.

The screws were set deep into the wood, too far for her fingers to reach and too far for her tools to be of any use. Tavera managed to keep the panic off her face as she realized this and she took Tender's face gingerly in her hands, his skin clammy to the touch. "I've got a bit of an issue here but I'll have you out as soon as I can, alright? Don't worry." She released his face when she was certain he could bear his own weight and picked the lock up off the ground, weighing it in her hands as she walked up to Kella.

"Kella, where do they keep the drivers for the bolts, for the stocks?" Kella turned around, her eyes still darting in her head as if she was expecting something to jump out at them. The priestess shook her head.

"Whoever is his overseer will have his keys," she whispered. "Someone is assigned to the people they keep here. They will have them." The priestess' head jerked up. Her eyes went wide as her body tensed with fear. "They're coming!"

Footsteps. As quickly as possible, she pulled the priestess aside and pressed herself flat against the wall, holding her breath as the steps drew closer. Kella did the same, her lips moving in silent prayer as the sound of one person walking stopped in front of the door. There was a jingling of keys and the door opened inward.

Tavera didn't wait to see who was within the robes. Lock in hand, she stepped forward. The figure started to turn. Bloodshot eyes went wide in amazement as Tavera drove the metal piece hard into his skull with all her might, unable to keep from grunting. He teetered there for a moment and she struck him again, the crunch of metal against bone sickening to hear. The man slumped to the ground, falling into Tender and knocked him off balance at first before he tipped forward. The wooden stock bounced and caught awkwardly on the floor, making Tender gag.

"Tender!" Tavera rushed over and helped him back up, looking to Kella with purpose in her voice. "The keys, get them!" They had been lucky. Kella scrambled toward the downed cultist, feeling around the robes and finding the keys on his belt. Tavera turned her head away as his hood fell back, the mutilated face of the man personalizing what she had just done.

It had been to help Tender, hadn't it? She had told herself that she would help him no matter what. She had at least been angry with Cy when she drew her blade and attacked him. She had struck this man out of fear. Her stomach was beginning to hurt, the feeling of striking him down still tingled in her hand. Tavera took the keys from Kella, finding the long, thin tool meant to draw out the bolts and screws. After a few tries and a few turns, the pins came unscrewed, loosening the stocks. Tavera pulled them off, setting them against the wall while keeping an eye on Tender. He stood on his own feet, swaying.

"You've freed me," he managed to mumble, his lips sticking together. His eyes looked dazed, but free from the weight of the stocks, a bit of energy seemed to seep into him. Tavera rubbed his shoulders quickly, trying to work the pain out of his muscles with her hands.

"I said I would," she said. She looked to Kella again, gesturing toward the body with a nod of the chin. "Get his robes off, and any weapons he has." Worry played on her nerves as she looked over him. "And I've done it. Like I said I would."

"I...don't really know you that well, do I?" he asked. Tavera smirked and put a hand on the side of his face.

"Not at all," she said. "You alright with that?"

"For now," Tender said. He took her hand in his and kissed the inside of her palm. "Thank you." He blinked a few times, the freedom from the stock seeming to invigorate his body and mind. With a grunt and a shudder he stood up from his seat, dipping his hand into what was left of the pitcher of water and running it over his face. Tavera looked to the stool he had been sitting on. With a few tugs, she managed to pull off one of the legs, handing it to Tender unceremoniously, but smiling.

"I am glad to see you're well, Sister Kella," he said, finally able to turn his attention to the woman. He bowed his head to the priestess, veering forward slightly as if he might fall but catching himself. He set his eyes on Tavera as he stretched his hand out, taking the robes from her and donning them. She offered him the sickle the man had had on him, but he held his hand up in refusal.

"We can still manage this." His voice sounded hoarse and his face looked like death but his eyes were bright and shining with a determination Tavera was glad to see. He looked toward the door and then back to the thief. "What is the plan?"

"A change in the plan is the plan." Tavera looked to the priestess and then to Tender, licking her lips before speaking, the sharp taste of blood on her tongue. "The priestess says there is another girl here, and that the cultists will probably kill her if we do not do anything."

"They will kill her, as they were going to kill me, Tender." There was an urgency in Sister Kella's voice. She held her hands together beseechingly as she stepped toward Tender. "We have to stop them, not just tonight--"

"I will try to put an end to this if I can, though the measure of it is daunting." He swayed slightly on his feet and Tavera rushed up to steady him, his full weight on her for a breath before he steadied himself. A slight smile tweaked at the corners of his mouth as he looked at Tavera for a moment, then nodded to the priestess. "I'm guessing this man came to get me for the ritual, to attend it as a part of my indoctrination. We have to assume Little and Gaela are close by, waiting to come to our aid. If we're to signal them in time to help us stop the ritual, we must go."

"Just pretend you're bringing us as your prisoners," Tavera said. "We'll try to find some chains on the way. I can make them appear tight but we'll be able to slip out of them." She looked to the priestess, seeing the troubled look on the older woman's face. "Do you know where we can get some chains, Sister?"

"I don't want to be tied up," the priestess half hissed, placing her hands on her face again, shaking her head as she spoke. "I don't want to go into the temple."

"Don't worry, we'll be safe. I promise, I'll get you out." Tender's voice was strained but his intonation was strong, his hand gripping the table leg as he spoke. "The community needs you. I won't let you die at the hands of those who would take advantage of you, Mistress." He stepped toward the door and took a deep breath as he wrapped his hand around the ring. "Stay behind me."

"Can you manage?" Tavera asked, not masking the concern she felt. Tender had only been freed a few moments ago. If the cultists had put him in the stocks as soon as they had arrived, it meant he had been in them for almost a day. She knew he was not the most skilled fighter, just the most zealous one. She wasn't sure if determination alone was going to carry him through this.

"I can," he said. He stood up straighter, the sound of spine bones cracking in the quiet cell. He looked over his shoulder and cast a wolfish smile at Tavera before pulling his hood up. "Can you manage to tie your bodice a bit tighter?"

Tavera snorted, shaking her head as she tightened the laces of the garment in question. Tender pulled the door open. Tavera raised a brow in surprise. He stepped out as if he was supposed to be leaving the cell, looking around before he disappeared, waving a hand as he did for them to follow. The thief supposed he was okay. His brush with danger had apparently sharpened his senses and though he move stiffly, he seemed alert. Having Tender back brought something like a smile to her face. Tavera tried to keep her head down, eyes to the ground in the event another cultist came upon them.

"There should be chains at the end of the hallway," Sister Kella said. She sounded irritated.

"We won't be chained for long," Tavera murmured, trying to reassure her again. The original plan had been to strike from behind. Though she hated that Tender hadn't listened to her and had endangered himself, as they picked their way through the menacingly quiet corridors, she had to admit she was glad to have him fighting at her side.

They crept through the corridors quietly, the eerie silence suggesting the ritual had already started. There were no windows, just halls of stone and brick. The temple was built into a cave, all the cells and storage areas carved into the tunnels lying beyond its sanctuary. Tavera looked around as they walked, trying to get a sense of direction, but just felt stone around her and something above her, something she wasn't sure they were ready for.

The cloying scent of incense wafted through the air, strong in some places. Just when Tavera thought they would get through the corridors undetected, the sound of a door opening set her teeth on edge and spun her around. A robed figure stepped into the hallway without locking the door. The figure froze when its hood faced them and the voice of an older woman escaped from within the robes.

"Where are you taking them?" the woman asked. Her low, shaky voice was laced more with curiosity more than suspicion. Tavera looked at Kella. The priestess' face was blank, eyes heavy-lidded, face void of emotion. The thief tried to duplicate the expression on her face, hoping she could pass for being unresponsive. Tender coughed, clearing his throat, trying to hide the table leg he carried behind him.

"I am taking them to see the ritual. I thought it only fitting." Tavera was impressed with how even he kept the tone of his voice. He must be frightened, hoping to avoid conflict and racking his brain for information that would make anything he said more believable. His overall confidence must have helped; the woman turned her head to the side, pulling back her hood to reveal her long, peppery hair and a wretched scar at her brow, her face creased to suggest she was older than Kella. She squinted at at them, pressing her lips together.

"He was glad to have you back, Mistress," she said to the priestess, her voice quaking slightly. She began to walk toward them and Tavera felt her own heart beat faster in her chest. Tender leaned back slightly as she approached, the woman standing before Kella. The old woman placed her hands on Kella's face, a tenderness in the gesture Tavera hadn't been expecting. The woman shook her head, her eyes filling with tears. "It is too bad he did not live long enough to see the avatar."

Tavera swallowed hard, the woman's news making her ears feel hot. She was the cause of Cy's death and this woman probably knew it. If she recognized Tavera as the killer of Cy, the woman didn't show it. What Tavera noticed was the look on Kella's face. It had gone from deliberate indifference to surprise, her mouth opening slightly. The old woman stroked her hair before pulling her to her chest, the way a mother might console her child.

"I know it has come as a shock, Kella. I have not told the others yet, and it is right that you are the first to know." Tavera noticed the look on Kella's face had changed to something darker and more sinister. Tavera could not bring herself to warn the old woman as she continued. "You are his first wife, the first bearer of the avatar. When they took you from us he was grief-stricken. We all were. And we vowed revenge on the church. Now, the new avatar will be here. She will prepare our bodies for the task of purging the land of fear and greed and hate--"

Sister Kella pushed back the older woman savagely. A loud growl hissed from her lips. There was a loud thump as the woman's head bounced on the stone floor. Before Tavera and Tender could see if she was alright, Kella leapt on top of her, her hands wrapped around the woman's throat. The priestess knocked the other woman's head against the floor, shrieking loudly. Alarmed, Tavera shot toward Sister Kella, reaching to grab her. A fist flew out at her, sending her back as pain shot across her face. Tender ducked in, placing a hand over Sister Kella's mouth and setting the table leg against her throat. He yanked her off of the other woman as she flailed and kicked, her muffled screams sounding too loud in the hall.

Tavera rushed over to where the old woman lay on the floor. Blood pooled behind her head. Her breathing was shallow, rasping. Claw marks raked red across her wrinkled skin where Sister Kella had dug in her nails. Without hesitating, Tavera wrapped her arms around the injured woman and pulled her down the hall toward the room she had exited from.

Inside, the wall was plastered with a large image of the corrupted aspect of the Goddess yet again, her calm face looking out toward the room giving it an eerie air. There was a large but simple bed in the room. Lying in the bed was the stiff figure of what used to be Cyric. His face looked waxy and his reddish hair seemed to have lost its luster. His eyes were closed. The white sheets were stained with red and brown, the bandages they had used to try and staunch the bleeding useless.

The smell of herbs was heavy in the room, a bowl of something green sitting on the chest that lay at the foot of the bed. A pitcher sat there as well; Tavera dropped the woman to the ground and rushed to it, hoping the head of the cult wasn't in need of the mind-altering brew they gave to would-be initiates.

It was water, fresh and cold. She splashed a bit into her hand, smelling it, letting the clear liquid run through her fingers. Tavera tipped it back toward her mouth. The taste of blood and dirt washed away and she gulped carefully, so as not to spill any of the precious liquid. As she drank she noticed the chest had no lock. Neither did the small box sitting at the altar built in front of the picture. She wiped her mouth with the back of her hand before she set the pitcher

down, too curious and her thievery too ingrained to not in-
spect the dead man's things.

The trunk had several robes in it and tunics, as well as a
pack. The clothing was quickly stuffed into the pack as she
threw one of the robes around her shoulders. A set of man-
acles lay at the bottom of the trunk. The keys were with
them. Tavera wondered what they were for, her eyes stray-
ing up toward the bed briefly as her stomach fluttered, her
mind blocking out the possibilities before stuffing these into
the bag as well.

She quickly turned her attention to the altar, finding several candles there. In the small drawer, a set of small knives
and other implements for cutting lay neatly arranged. A vial
of some dreadful-smelling liquid lay next to them, probably
meant to keep them free from sickness. These were also
taken. The door opened behind her. Tavera glanced back,
not surprised to see Tender and Sister Kella entering the
room.

"Point!" Tender hissed. The sound of someone climbing
into the bed drew Tavera's attention away from the altar. Sister Kella had thrown herself over the body of Cy, as a wife
might be expected to do of her husband. But the priestess'
visage was hard, a mixture of emotions pulling at her face.
Tavera stood up, fixing her new cloak as Tender eyed her,
shaking his head.

"How could you take his things?" he asked. His eyes
drifted toward the dead man. There was still a hint of fear
on his face, as if he expected him to sit up in bed. Tavera
shrugged, throwing the pack on and pulling the cloak on
over it so that it looked as if her back was hunched.

"He's dead. He can't use them anymore. Ain't it the custom, to divide the goods of the dead? I'm just...keeping custom." Tavera picked the pitcher of water off the floor and

held it out toward Tender. "He ain't using this either. You want it?" Tender peered in, his eyes growing wide as he realized what was there, relief washing over his face as he guzzled the cool water. He set the pitcher on the closed chest, looking to the priestess. She hadn't moved but her eyes were closed. Tender placed a hand on the woman's shoulder. Sister Kella jumped, startled.

"Mistress, we should go." Tender's voice was low and sympathetic, and the priestess allowed him to help her off the bed. Her robes were stained now with red blood. Cy's blood and the dirt of the prison. Sister Kella looked down at her robes a wry smile forming on her face. Tender looked toward the closed door. "We have to go if we are going to save the girl."

"If Hira is still in the compound, the girl is still whole." Kella's voice was void of emotion, her face still shadowed as she kept her gaze on the floor. "She is their 'healer.'" She spat the words, her sarcasm thick as she looked at the unconscious old woman on the floor. Blood had pooled under her head here as well. "She oversees the ritual. She performs the physical part while the priest performs the spiritual. And the others look on, praying and chanting. Their blood pouring to join hers." Sister Kella looked down at her garments, soiled with blood. She shook her head and removed them, stripping down to the simple grey-and -reen dress she wore underneath. "They are all probably waiting for her in the temple, waiting for her to come with her knives and her herbs and her lack of pity." She looked up at them both, the hatred on her face dark. "If it had gotten close, they would have come for her."

"Even still, we must leave," Tender managed to say after a silence which had gone too long. He put an arm around the priestess' shoulder, leading her out of the room, Tavera following behind. Sister Kella pulled away from his arm suddenly, facing them both, her face pale, making her eyes shine more brightly in the low lamplight.

"Which one of you did it?" she asked, her voice quavering as she brought her hand to her mouth. Her eyes darted back and forth between them, searching their faces and lingering too long on them both. Tender started to say something but Tavera spat the words out before he lied.

"I did." The priestess stared at her. Tavera held her breath, expecting the woman to fly at her. But Kella only nodded, pressing her lips together before she turned around and opened the door.

"He was responsible for Wing's death," she said as they stepped out into the hallway, her voice low and steady as she measured her words. "He didn't slit her throat, but he made Wing...do what she did." Tavera thought back to the illustration in the journal, of the body on the floor. It must have been Wing. A smear of red at her throat, a shard of something in her hand. "He and Hira and the others who were there then," Sister Kella said, her voice less shaky than Tavera thought it would be.

As they walked down the corridor, Tavera heard the door to the dead man's cell close. The priestess' shoulders rose slightly at the definitive sound. "He was responsible for killing the only person I loved freely," she continued, her voice threatening to break. Sister Kella remained firm as she made the admission, leading them down the hall toward the temple. "And though I was bound to him, and loved him as I was made to love him, I hated him more. I wish I could have killed him. He took my life from me and gave me only pain in return."

A pang of guilt hit Tavera as the priestess spoke, the woman's hands clenched in anguish. In a way she had stolen something from Sister Kella with a simple push of her blade. But hadn't Tavera taken much more than that, when she ended Cyric's life? Tavera felt worse about taking Kella's revenge, but knew killing him had been the right choice. Tender looked as if he was about to say something but he bowed his head and held his tongue. There was no appropriate response, except to follow behind her and hope that Little and Gaela would be there when they needed them.

Chapter 17
Bloody Work

Tavera had seen many things over the course of her life. She had seen the effects of diseases on the body. Once or twice she had seen people beaten to death. Heard the sounds of bones breaking and blood spurting. She had encountered people driven mad from facing death, left with no choice but to wither away within their own heads and wander through life like a ghost. What Tavera saw in the sanctuary of the Temple of the Red Moon Rising was not as horrific, but the bizarreness of the scene was to stay with her for many phases to come.

Half-naked cultists moved throughout the open room, hot, red blood gleaming on their sweaty bodies. Though there weren"t more than two dozen individuals, the sound of their prayers and shrieking reverberated through the incense-laden air. It made the hair on the back of Tavera's neck stand up. Arms and legs flailed, blood splattering around as their eyes rolled back in their heads, the torchlight glinting off the sticky crimson liquid. No music played in the temple but the praying had a melodic, yet off key quality to it, like a familiar song played too quickly and out of tune.

Tavera's eyes trailed over the ghastly scene. The wall behind the altar was painted with a mural of the bloody Goddess. Smears of blood dripped on the wall, crimson hand prints and long trails strangely reminiscent of scarlet flowers with long stems, the hand-prints fanning out beneath the terrible Goddess like a war-torn field. The wretched plate which had been the start of all this trouble sat on top of a white stone altar.

Sitting on a throne behind the altar was a very dazed, pregnant young woman. Her large belly protruded from her abdomen, the skin smooth and taut with the child resting within her. Her head rested on her own shoulder as if her neck had no strength. Her chest heaved, her eyes unfocused on the scene in front of her. Tavera's eyes went wide, looking to Kella from within her hood. Kella nodded and then looked up, her eyes pointing toward the skylight in the ceiling. The moon would tell them when the ceremony began.

"So, why did we walk into the middle of this?" Tavera whispered, drawing closer to Tender.

"Too confident, too stupid?" Tender answered, a hint of a squeak in his voice.

"I do believe it's too late to back away slowly," Tavera muttered, wishing she was in the hallway. Her stomach turned as one of the cultists approached them. He was younger than Cy, probably just a few years older than Tender. His rough black robes were pulled down and tied about his waist exposing his sweaty chest. Long lines of red gore streamed down his torso. His face was smeared red as well, his one eye shimmering with energy, blood collecting in the ragged scar that ran down the side of his face. As he set his eye on Tavera, his expression dropped. He looked confused and then horrified. He stepped back in an exaggerated way, recoiling in terror. "You are not Cyric!" His shriek, roused some from their ecstatic stupors, the volume in the room dropping. "What have you done with our High Priest?"

Tavera looked down at her robes. "Tits," she cursed, realizing all too late that by taking robes from his trunk, she had probably made herself out to be the leader of the cultists. By this time, all the bloodied people were looking towards the three of them. Some looked confused by their presence. Others looked around the temple, as if surprised to be there. Tavera looked at the floor for a second before her mouth popped open, a quick lie at the tip of her tongue but Tender pushed past her, pulling his hood back for all to see.

"Cyric is dead!" he shouted, addressing the crowd. He waited for a moment as his statement rolled over their ears, the people looking at each other. "He is dead. He was killed, and you know how. He bled to death from his wound. While I realize now this might not be an altogether bad thing to you people," Tender said, looking around the room. No one was moving. Tavera didn't think she could move now if she wanted to. "He is still dead," Tender continued. "Your leader is gone. You have no one to guide you down your errant path.

"What you are doing here is WRONG." He said the word so loud Tavera jumped. He took another step forward, the fire in his eyes rivaling that of the torchlight. "You are kidnapping people, in the name of your depraved and horrible Goddess! This aspect you revere, it is disgusting and manipulative. It is willing to poison the minds of people for worship, thirsty for blood and hungry for sacrifices from the unwilling!" At this, he pointed his table leg at the pregnant girl. For the first time, Tavera realized she had no weapons.

The twenty or so cultists were starting to stir, looking to one another. Several started walking towards them.

Tender seemed oblivious to everything not in their favor about this situation. As he spoke, a slight breeze seemed to waft through the room. "I am urging you, in the name of the good Bosom, to turn from this evil and to live lives that do not harm other people or yourselves. And for the love of Tits, Little, I hope you're out there!"

Their backs were to the altar now, at the base of the steps leading up to the platform. They were surrounded. Tavera heard Sister Kella praying under her breath; she didn't dare take her eyes off the crowd starting to press in on them. Faces were twisted with rage and offense. Some of them growled, bloodied saliva dripping from their mouths as they gnashed their teeth. Tender grabbed Tavera by the arm and put himself in front of her, urging her toward the pregnant girl. His knuckles were white as his hand gripped the table leg. "Point, get her loose. Sister, stay behind me. Little, HURRY UP!"

Tavera ran up the steps to the altar, her breath tight in her chest as she rushed to the side of the girl. She heard shrieks, the cultists' cries even worse than their worship. A single cry was cut short as the smack of wood against flesh and bone ended it. Tender grunted. Tavera felt something behind her and looked out into the rest of the temple. A shimmer of a shadow in one of the corners tightened and turned into the point of a blade, the forms of Little and Gaela emerging.

Little said nothing but charged noiselessly forward, his blade a low, shining arch as it swept upward and across the back of a cultist. The haggard-looking old man screamed in pain but wheeled around to face him. Tavera gulped, wanting to watch Gaela and Little, wanting to help them fight back. But the girl was first.

She was surprised to see the pregnant girl was young, younger than Tavera. If she hadn't known any better she would have thought the girl was inebriated. Incense burned, thick and sticky, making the girl cough. All along the start of her scalp were the telltale scars. One of her scars was jagged, broken. She had resisted at some point. The pregnant girl wasn't bleeding and both her eyes were intact. Her hands were free and her dark, long hair covered her face, as if her head had fallen forward with sleepiness. "Hey," Tavera said, trying to stay calm. "Hey, wake up. Rise and shine. First meal time." The girl picked her head up slowly, her eyes fluttering open. "Whatever you're on, I could probably get a pretty grip for it in the 'Wicks," Tavera tried to joke, smacking the girl lightly across the face. Her pupils were so dilated Tavera couldn't tell what color the irises were. "Tits," Tavera cursed, trying not to think of what the cultists were going to do to this girl in this state. Behind them was the altar, the plate laid out with various knives and other sharp instruments. Tavera racked her brain on how to wake up the girl.

The bottle of vile-smelling liquid. Maybe that would work. Tavera threw the pack to the ground and rummaged for what seemed like far too long. There was a rumble and a crash behind her. "To Her Hems with you!" she heard Tender curse, followed by the sounds of fists and kicks. Tavera pried the stopper off, putting it under the girl's nose and moving it around. The girl's head jerked up suddenly, revealing drowsy eyes. They focused on Tavera for a moment, then jerked to the side, looking at something that was apparently drawing closer.

Tavera stood up and wheeled around in time to face the cultist running toward her, his blood-splattered body making her cringe. She ducked as he dove for her, sinewy, blood-stained arms outstretched. "You will not take her from us," he shrieked, diving at her again, arms flailing. She dodged out of his grasp, rolling off of him before kicking him squarely on his backside, pushing him down and to the ground. He screamed in pain this time, his knees driving into the stone of the temple stage.

"Toss off, I'm trying to do just that," Tavera joked nervously. She set her feet firmly on the ground, waiting for him to attack. The cultist scrambled up, grabbing one of the tools from the altar. Tavera reached for her own, gulping as she remembered she was unarmed.

"You shall be purged and we will have our avatar!" He screamed again as he rushed forward. Tavera stepped aside and tripped him, hoping he would stay down this time or at least be discouraged. She kicked him hard in the stomach, not able to help but snarl as her boot made contact with his gut.

The man gasped and coughed as he clutched his midsection. Tavera turned around to deal with the pregnant girl but felt the man rise behind her. She turned around quickly to face him. "I'd stay down, if I were you," she threatened, trying to focus on him and not the swinging swords and arms in the temple. His eyes gave away his plan before he executed it. The cultist rushed the girl in the seat, his arm raised to strike her with the knife.

It was Tavera's turn to rush him. She leapt forward, intending to shove him with her shoulder. Perhaps a trip down the stairs would stay his hand. But he raised the knife to defend himself, so Tavera had to change plans. As the man dodged, the knife sliced across her hands and arms, barely missing her face by a hands'-width. Still Tavera managed to grab hold of his wrists. The cultist struggled. He moved the knife, trying to slice at her wrist, teeth bared. She saw the muscle and sinew in his arms ripple as he pushed against her and Tavera strained against him, her adrenaline posing only some match for his zeal for the Goddess.

"Do not resist," the cultist hissed. His blue eyes were intent upon her and he spit when he spoke. "I have already begun the process on you." Tavera winced, feeling the cuts on her hands and arms burn as she fought him, blood dripping down her skin. "Do you not feel the filth of your self draining from you?" he hissed. "Ecstasy awaits as the body is purged and the spirit comes forward. Fear will be forgotten, regrets. Do you not wish this?"

Tavera eyed the sharp blade one more time before she shifted her weight, ramming her knee into his groin. He doubled over and she head-butted him as hard as she dared. The man slumped to the ground, clutching his groin, the knife at his side. Tavera kicked him in the gut again, stars circling in her eyes.

"Chew Her Hems and stay down," she mumbled, picking the knife up off the ground. Out of the corner of her eye she saw two cultists rushing her way. Without hesitating she threw the knife at one. The blade sunk into the man's belly, his hands wrapping around the hilt of the blade while he grimaced terribly. The woman still advanced. Tavera balled her fists, ready for a fight when the woman fell forward, as if struck squarely between the shoulder blades. The woman's face twisted in pain, though no sound escaped her mouth as she fell forward.

As the woman fell away, Tavera spied Gaela, her hands spread in some arcane gesture. Tavera watched as Gaela stamped her foot, then slid it across the ground. A ripple of motion shot its way toward a half-naked man waving his arms wildly at Little. As the force hit him, he toppled over, almost falling onto Tender's brother, who let out a string of impressive curses. Tavera raised her eyebrows at Gaela before getting back to the girl. The girl seemed more coherent now. "Come on now," Tavera said. "Time for us to calmly slip away while those folk do the hard work." Tavera snaked an arm under her shoulder, helping her up.

She looked over the room, noticing Tender and Little were drawing most of the attention. The barkeep had sufficiently enraged them with his speech and Little made a good show of his sword work. The cultists seemed afraid of Gaela. Her hand gestures drew curses from them but they didn't draw near, deciding to take on the two physical foes instead. Sister Kella stayed at Gaela's side. She couldn't tell if Kella was afraid to fight or afraid to start fighting. Tavera hoped Tender and Little would give her the chance to slip out with the girl.

She glanced toward the plate, noticing a hint of red light shining on the silvered surface. Tavera looked up quickly, shifting the girl's weight as her eyes went big, the red cusp of the full moon starting to make its way into view through the skylight.

The eclipse was happening. Had the moment to perform the ceremony passed entirely?

The fight raged on. Tender and Little were splattered with blood. Whether it was their own or from the cultists, Tavera couldn't tell. Gaela moved her hands and two cultists fell head over heels, crying out in pain. If Tavera could get the girl out before the eclipse was over, perhaps the bloodshed would end.

A shrill cry escaped from the throat of one of the cultists. Tavera wheeled around to see where the threat came from. An older man with stringy hair, his pale face streaked with the red of blood and firelight, pointed at them with a bony, gnarled hand. "You shall not take her from us!

You shall not deny us our avatar!" he shrieked. A strange quiet stretched through the temple as he reached within his robes. What he drew out made Tavera catch her breath, her heart pounding in her chest. It was a sickle, like the one Cy had used when he cast his spell on her.

The old man flourished the curved blade and Tavera felt her skin crawl. She stepped back, the silver metal starting to glow as his lips spoke words she could not hear. "Point!" Tender shouted as he rammed his shoulder into the adversary he was fighting, throwing her aside. He hurled himself at the old man just as the ball of light licked off the tip of the blade.

The ball seemed to shoot toward Tavera in slow motion, her eyes starting to cross as she followed its straight path. She had been hit by one of these before. What had the cultists talked about? Fear, purging, freedom. What had the spell done before? It had made her face her greatest regret and her greatest fear. The light came closer. Her mind buzzed, though her body wouldn't move.

Out of the corner of her eye, she saw the plate glow red, the full moon's light pouring into it from above. Her fears, her regrets, could she give them up? Or would she fall victim to them all the rest of her life? She closed her eyes as the ball of light struck her with a force not felt by her skin but by her mind. The same pain seeped through her eyes, nose and mouth. It swam around her head, trying to wrap itself around something, some thought.

Tavera's head jerked back and her grip on the girl loosened. She fell to the ground, her hands going to her face to try and pry the pain out of her head. Her breath came in short gasps as the light danced within her eyes, but she forced her mind to push her dark thoughts out, purging them herself before the light had its way with her mind. No regrets, no fears.

What was done had been done. Stabbing Lori, leaving Derk, keeping secrets from Tender…they had not been selfish acts, any of them, though to an outside eye they might seem that way. She knew they weren't. Her head hit the ground, bouncing against the cold stone. She smiled as Tender drove Little's sword into the side of the old man, his eyes aglow with triumphant rage. The man slumped down to the ground, his open mouth foaming with blood and spittle.

The last thing she saw was Tender running for her, his bloody hands stretched toward her as he mouthed her name.

Chapter 18
No Regrets

The sound of scraping chairs, a raucous singer and a bar-keep's shouts of orders mingled with the aroma of frying bread and stewing rabbits. This was fine by Tavera. She was lost in her thoughts, wondering what the strange dream she'd had the night before meant. In her dream, she was naked and standing with the man who had led the cere-mony of her initiation into the Cup. They were kissing when suddenly she was wheeled around. A woman stood in front of her, an elven woman with long dark hair and sad eyes. The woman smiled as she placed a crown on Tavera's head and when she did, thousands of elves came into view be-hind her.

They stood, their ears growing, large and wide, and when they were as big as they were tall, the elves' ears began to flap, like the wings of a bat. One by one, they began to flit up into the air, flying up and away. The woman also flew up, holding her hand out but Tavera's ears hadn't both grown. Only one had, while the injured one remained small. The large ear flapped, lifting her part-way off the ground but

Tavera flew in circles, unable to get anywhere. All of the elves fluttered away into a forest of green-and-white leaves, dappled light seeming to swallow them as they flew farther and farther away. The woman watched her with haunting eyes as she flew backward until she was out of sight.

A mug of ale was set before Tavera, rousing her from her thoughts. Her eyes caught Tender's and he smiled at her from across the table, sitting backward on his chair before taking a swig of his ale.

"How is it?" she asked, staring down into her mug. Tender smacked his lips, looking to the side as he analyzed the taste, taking another swig and swishing it around in his mouth before giving his verdict.

"Not as good as mine, but not half bad," he said, setting his mug down on the table. "But hey, this drink is practically free, so I won't be overly harsh."

"I can't believe you tried to turn down the money from Sister Fera's father," Tavera laughed, some of her seriousness melting away. "You've a lot to learn. If a man offers you a reward for returning his pregnant daughter after her being missing for a year, you take it!"

"Her temple offered us room and board for no cost, didn't they?" Tender said. "They were glad to have the young sister back."

"Free food from a temple ain't pay, Tender," Tavera sighed, resting her chin in her hand. "It's charity. Charity for hard work. We were dealt a hardship and we dealt with it well, considering. I'd like a bit more than a bowl of soup after my sword eats a bit."

"Well, we didn't do it for money, Point, we did it…because it was the right thing to do." He took another, slower sip from his cup as he looked at her, biting his top lip. "You…do you agree?"

"Of course I do." It had been the right thing to do. "No regrets. We couldn't rescue Kella just to have Fera turn out like her or worse." Tavera finally managed to drink her ale, making a face as she swallowed. "This ale is too watery, Tender, how dare you say it was fine?"

"There's a law about the contents of the beer in this town," he said, draining his cup and setting it down with a bang on the table top. "Something about moderation...I dunno." He shrugged, looking at her cup. "You don't like it?"

"Ah, it's...it's fine." She took another gulp, stifling a grimace as she swallowed and feigning a smile as she looked to Tender. He hadn't shaved in a while and his face was starting to catch up with his mustache, his dark eyes still merry in the light of the tavern.

"I know you just miss Tender's drinks, you do." He smiled and winked at her, taking her mug from her and downing it. Tavera just laughed, drumming her fingers on the table top. Her face became serious again as thoughts of the previous phase swam around her mind.

"Do you think...do you think Kella will find her child?" Tavera blinked as she spoke, finding the words harder to say than she thought. As much as she had figured out reading Kella's journals and interacting with the cult, what they had learned afterward had been more astonishing. Cyric had not only been her husband but the father of a child Sister Kella had seen for a brief instant before her fellow priestesses had whisked it away. The older priestess had been rescued years ago in the last stage of her pregnancy. Tavera remembered Sister Kella's face as she recounted the ordeal. Members of the church had insisted her child could not stay with its mother. Sister Kella's face had darkened when she let slip the sinister truth. Some of the older members had even insisted the child should not live.

All these arguments had been made in the weeks leading up to the child's birth, the decision withheld from Sister Kella until days after she had delivered, when she was wracked with grief at the thought of her child being killed by the church she had served all these years. Years later, Kella had been sent to Tender's community as a kind of retirement, along with the plate she had almost fallen victim to. The cultists, who had reorganized, would not think to find it with her. They church had been wrong and Tavera and Tender and everyone else had to come to the rescue.

Tender shrugged, looking down into the cup with his brows furrowed, as though thoughts he did not wish to entertain had entered his mind. "I don't know," he said. "The priestesses seemed...I didn't expect them to act like that." He shook his head, rubbing the side of his nose with his hand, catching the eye of the bartender and signaling for two more drinks. "They seemed more upset at the situation than I thought. They seemed happy enough to have Fera back and but they were just cold to Kella."

"Most churches show kindness to their congregations. But..." Tavera's voice trailed off as she thought about the right thing to say. She thought about the things Derk would say to her, how they would argue though they loved each other. She remembered Derk and Old Gam's voices in the night, low and sharp and then other sounds. "People that're close, they're the ones who hurt us the most. There's probably a lot of ruffled feathers between them."

Tender leaned back in his chair. Tavera tried to catch his gaze but couldn't, the bartender-turned-rescuer tracing wet rings on the wooden table top with his finger. "She didn't mean to get kidnapped by the cult. The church just wanted to put her away. Away in the Freewild. With me and Little." Tender nodded as a server set two mugs in front of them.

Tender watched the person go before he leaned in, his voice low and deep as he spoke. "Did you know about Kella? About the child?"

"No." She said it quickly, hoping it didn't sound guilty. Tavera shook her head, running her finger around the edge of her mug, pressing her lips together as she did. "I didn't. I mean, I guessed maybe something like that had happened to her when I saw Fera. But there was nothing about it in her journals." Tavera thought back to all the ink-stained pages, blotted out with black and red. "I knew about Wing, in a way. Sister Kella filled in the rest." She took a gulp of the watery ale, trying not to think on the torment Sister Kella must have faced. Again, the bottles of liquor the priestess drank made sense.

"Why didn't you tell me more about what was in the journals?" There was a touch of accusation in Tender's voice and it caught Tavera's attention, her spine straightening as she sat up in her chair.

"I didn't want you to get scared off," she said. "Or overzealous. I knew you cared about Sister Kella. If you knew what might be happening to her, what they could do, you might get scared or worse, blinded. You had purpose. It didn't need zeal or emotion added to it."

"Emotion." He chuckled, his eyes growing darker as he looked down at the table, the previous merriment draining from his face.

"What do you feel right now?" Tavera asked, quietly.

"So many things," Tender said, rubbing his face with his hand. "Glad we all made it out of there. Worried about Sister Kella. Disap--" His voice cut off. Tender paused for a moment, taking a gulp of his beer. He wouldn't look Tavera in the eye. "I ran someone through with a sword. Because I was angry."

"We were in danger, Tender," Tavera said.

"I grabbed Little's sword from him and cut a man down," he said.

"And I thank you for doing it," Tavera said. They sat there quietly, Tavera trying to grasp at what to say next. "You killed him so he couldn't do anything worse to anyone, to me. I was unconscious, unarmed. Is that what you want? My thanks?"

"No," Tender said. He put his head in his hands for a moment and took a deep breath.

"Well, good," Tavera said. "Good people and bad are killed every day, Braxton. Killed by good people and bad people. For all sorts of reasons. Remember, you're...you're one of the good ones, Tender."

Tender looked at her. Did he believe her? Tavera didn't know if she could say the same about herself. She didn't feel like she could. It didn't bother her to know it. It only bothered her that others might figure it out and try to stop her. Tender didn't seem interested in Tavera's goodness at the moment. "Are you doing okay?" he asked.

"Yeah," was all she managed to say, her voice trailing off. She took a sip of her watery beer, trying to fill the pit in her stomach. "Look, Tender. I came along with you to rescue the sister to help. Do you think I did?"

Tender glanced over at her, pressing his lips together for a moment before he nodded. "You did. You got the priestess out of the cell, which I imagine you would have managed alone, had I trusted you." He grimaced momentarily, taking a sip of his beer before setting his dark eyes on her, leaning in close again. "Do you even understand why I went in after you? Why I followed you to the bar?"

"Tender, look, it's behind us. I don't care that you didn't trust me, it worked out in the end, didn't it?"

"It wasn't lack of trust," he said quickly, interrupting her before she could speak. Tavera sat back in her chair, waiting for Tender's mouth to form the words he wanted to say. "It's, it's…I was worried about you. You didn't say much about your part in the plan, or how you were going to get the priestess out of her cell, just that you would. I know now what you are. A thief. Not just one of those people living by luck, traveling from town to town, going by their wits. I saw you take those things from Cyric, I saw you break open the locks of the stock, I saw you drive your sword into that man…." Tender shook his head, looking down at the table. "The look on your face…."

"Did you like what you saw?" Her sarcasm seemed to dry her mouth and she took another sip of her watery ale, sinking down in her chair. Tavera narrowed her eyes slightly at Tender, trying to read the various emotions playing on his face. His brows knit together for a moment, his face relaxing as he looked at her, the same good face she had first encountered looking into her eyes.

"I want to know you," he said finally. "I want to know who you are. That is what I saw when you first walked into my bar, a person to be unraveled. You looked so mischievous and yet so sad, but sweet at the same time." Tender moved his chair out and swung it so it landed next to Tavera, sitting in the chair backward again. "I mean, come on…I don't even know your real name!"

He took her hand in his and leaned on the table, a smile playing under his mustache. "I know it isn't Point, it can't be. We're friends, right? We fought alongside one another. Maybe not literally but we just did this…unbelievable thing together! We escaped from prison! We saved two people from death and mutilation. It's the kind of thing the storytellers go on about around fires, or priestesses wax on at prayers."

"Maybe you should work it into your sermon, next time you run vespers," Tavera said with an easy smile. He laughed now and Tavera too, the two friends taking a moment to consider the enormity of what they had just done and the absurdity of how it had all worked out. Tavera watched Tender's face as it grew more serious for a moment, and he squeezed her hand gently. He lowered his voice so she had to lean in to hear him, going along with his usual ploys to seem endearing, which was endearing in itself. "So, come on," he said. "Tell me something. About yourself."

Tavera could give him a fake name, make something up off the top of her head and say it with a straight face and leave it at that. It would pacify Tender, but she knew she would regret lying to him and she refused to have things weighing down her conscience anymore. Would having someone call her by her name be such a bad thing?

Derk had always said to be careful about who knew who you really were, especially people you were unsure of yourself. But Tender wouldn't use anything he knew about her against her, she was sure of that, and Tender was one of the easiest people to read she had ever met. The thought of someone's voice that wasn't Derk's saying those three syllables, though…she shook her head, surprised to find her face was hot and her eyes stung as she tried not to cry. "I…I was born outside of the 'Wicks. Is that…is that enough?"

"If that's what you'll give me, I will take it gladly." Tender brought her hand to his mouth and kissed the top of it before standing, still refusing to let go of her hand. "Let's go find my brother and his new best friend, eh?" Tavera took a deep breath as she stood also, hooking her arm through his as they left the bar.

Tender pulled some money out of his belt pouch, flicking it onto the bar top so it spun on its side when it landed, and smiled at the exasperated barkeep who had seen all kinds of tricks with coins before. Tavera leaned her head against Tender's arm as they walked out, thinking about what she had told him, wondering why Tender was so patient with her, so adamant about knowing her...and why she liked it so much. She pulled away from him long enough to pull up her hood, another spring rain pouring down from the gray clouds.

"It's weird, them being friends, eh?" Tender shook his head, his dark eyes squinting as he tried to see past the rain drops to the street. Tavera shrugged against him, looking down at their feet as they walked the muddy road.

"I guess it ain't too strange," she mused. Tavera chuckled within her hood, thinking of something Little had said to Gaela. "Though the joke he made about them two, what an idiot. I was shocked when she laughed at it. I thought she was going to knock him over for half a breath."

Tender laughed too, stopping under a stoop and looking around the corner. "True enough, my brother is not the... the cleverest. Or the best with words." Tender looked up and down the street, frowning slightly. "Where did they say they were going again?"

"The glass store," Tavera said. She stood up straighter and started to pull Tender on the right course, smiling at him as he realized he had been going to wrong way. "Gaela wanted to buy some things with our reward money, and Little was going to help her with the bargaining. Why did she--?"

"Good luck to her," Tender laughed. Tavera led him around a rather large puddle, rain making it past the confines of her hood and splashing onto her face. Spring was nice but summer was better, she thought. Once the rains had washed everything away, the sun would shine and make everything green and warm. Sleeping outdoors would be more comfortable and though the days would be long, the nights would be vibrant.

They walked by another bar, the music a band was playing sounding melodiously over the gentle rushing of the rain. Tender took her hand and spun her around, trying to seem dashing as he attempted to lead her in a silly dance on the side of the road. Tavera laughed, rolling her eyes at his antics. "If you want to impress me with dancing, you'll have to do better than that," she chuckled, still willing to dance in the street. He took her hands in his and bowed at the knee before he raised an eyebrow at her, spinning her around and pulling her close so her back was against his chest. Tavera looked at their fingers laced together, his face close to hers.

"Will you come back with us?" he asked. Tavera pulled away from Tender, looking to the ground. The music of the band faded away as they continued down the street. Several children darted out from around a corner, almost knocking them over but stopping just in time before they darted away in another direction, their laughter warm despite the chill of the storm. Tender walked alongside her, easily keeping pace. "I think we did something good together. And if we work together more, we'll figure each other out and help some people in the process. We did a fairly good job. We could do good things."

"You mean you could get us into scrapes and I can make sure you get paid?" She smirked, the idea sounding not altogether bad. However, the thought of Tender killing the man with a sword...she had seen it in his face back at the bar. It still bothered him. The thought of him accumulating regrets because of her was something she couldn't tolerate. Tavera stopped in the street, forcing Tender to stop with her. It was time to come up with a story, and a believable one.

"Look, this was a good thing we did, but I'm not sure I'll always be of use to you. You'll probably go back to tending bar and well, I get anxious sitting around. You want me winning all of those farmers' monies?" She smiled at him, realizing what she was saying wasn't a story but true. She couldn't go back to Whitend. There was nothing there for her to do and as much as she liked hanging around his bar, it had been boring after a few days. Tender shook his head.

"I don't want you to be of use, I want to work with you," Tender said. "I can find you something to keep you busy. We could...you could tend my bar!" Tavera laughed out loud, putting her hands in her pockets and continuing down the street, still laughing when he caught up to her. "Come on, you can't tell me you want to flit from town to town, getting into trouble?"

"I don't get into trouble, I just make it and then flit off," she grinned, walking faster toward the store. Tender jogged alongside her, trying to keep up.

"Look, stop!" He grabbed her arm and spun her around, putting his arms on her shoulders as he panted, rain dripping off of his hair. "Look, leave, fine but promise me you'll stop by before summer." Tender looked up into the air as if he was looking for his words there, finally meeting her gaze. "Promise me, I'll find something for us to do, us four. What do you say?"

Tender's eyes shone so bright and his face looked so hopeful it almost made Tavera blush. "Fine," she finally relented, sighing. Tender wrapped his arm around her shoulders again and walked with her down the street. "But don't go stirring up trouble just to get me to come along, I won't have it!"

"I wouldn't dream of it," Tender said. They walked with his arm around her shoulder until they reached the glass store. Tavera didn't bother to shrug him off. It was chilly and Tender was warm and he smelled good. She wouldn't give it more thought than that.

ABOUT THE AUTHOR

Tristan is a novelist, comic book writer, and freelance RPG writer and she used to write the weekly column 'Reality Makes the Best Fantasy' for the roleplaying site Troll in the Corner.

As a fan of speculative fiction the first fantasy book she fell in love with was The Crystal Cave.

Originally hailing from New York City, she considers Portland, OR her home and resides with her spouse, Small Boss, a cat that knows it's a Multipass and Azrael.

OTHER BOOKS

The Valley of Ten Crescents Series
Little Girl Lost
Thieves at Heart
Self-Made Scoundrel

Short Stories
Botanica Blues

Anthologies
Allegories of the Tarot

LITTLE GIRL LOST

TRISTAN J. TARWATER

A Valley of Ten Crescents Tale

THIEVES AT HEART

TRISTAN J. TARWATER

The Valley of Ten Crescents Book One

TRISTAN J. TARWATER

SELF-MADE
SCOUNDREL

The valley of Ten crescents book Two

A MODERN LOVECRAFTIAN TALE OF TERROR

BOTANICA BLUES

TRISTAN J. TARWATER